Alex is part of Earth's last hope: a crew member on a ship sent out from a dying planet, wishing for a second chance. He wakes from his cryo pod to find destruction. Their mission has failed, he and his commander, Luke Belka, are the only ones to survive the journey.

Luke insists that help must be coming, that one of the other ships on the mission must also have reached this planet. Whether or not he's right, they will need to survive on this lush alien planet. And maybe find happiness along the way.

ABUNDANCE

Emmalynn Spark

A NineStar Press Publication

Published by NineStar Press
P.O. Box 91792,
Albuquerque, New Mexico, 87199 USA.
www.ninestarpress.com

Abundance

Copyright © 2019 by Emmalynn Spark
Cover Art by Natasha Snow Copyright © 2019

Printed in the USA
First Edition
March, 2019

Print ISBN: 978-1-950412-29-7

Also available in eBook, ISBN: 978-1-950412-13-6

Warning: This book contains sexually explicit content, which may only be suitable for mature readers.

For Hils, who read this story when it was only ideas on note cards and said "Yeah, I'd read that."

Chapter One

I BLINKED AWAKE groggily. Around me, there were urgent noises that I knew were important, but none of them quite caught my attention and, when I tried to twitch my arms and my legs, they weren't moving right.

I drifted up two, three times. The last time, I was aware enough to know I was still in the pod. Still hooked up to the machine that breathed for me. Still drifting in fluid. There was an alarm. Someone should turn it off. Someone would be by shortly to let me out. I was probably low priority.

I drifted back to sleep.

I woke again.

Things were sharper this time. The alarm, for one. The mist in my brain that'd held it away was receding, and now its panicked shrieking was piercing right through. I wriggled a little, happy to find I could. My limbs were listening again, admittedly in a jerky way. I was cold, still. So cold.

Something was very, very wrong. I tried to parse it, but my brain was like cotton wool. Thoughts tripped over themselves, half started then drifted away as I tried to really bring them into focus, then danced about the corners of my mind. Something wasn't right but it seemed distant. Surreal.

Then, slowly, one thing shifted into focus. Whatever the emergency, I shouldn't have been left so long.

I shouldn't have been waking up alone. The ship triggered all the pods to begin defrost when we made landfall on New Earth, but someone should have been up before me. Something should have been opening the pod for me, easing me into this new world. Command and medical were meant to be up first, then those with training to be first boots on the ground. The other science staff and I were way down the list of priorities.

Still, they'd planned for this kind of thing. I'd been trained for this. I jerked my hand out, unhappy at how erratically and clumsily it moved. Maybe it was just too soon. Maybe I should just stay in my pod.

But why the alarm? Why hadn't anyone shut off the alarm?

Eventually, my numb and twisted fingers found the emergency release. It was a task to get them to curl around the handle, but I did, and I pulled.

There was a popping, a release, then a slightly raising of the lid above me. I reached up and shoved at it. It moved easily, sliding like it'd been closed yesterday. Of course it did, no air in space. No corrosion. But it also meant I couldn't have been on the planet for long either, as our best guess was that New Earth had breathable air.

If it didn't, we were all doomed anyway.

The fluid began to leak out of the cracks and I shoved at the lid again, opening it more. The movement sent jolts of pain through my limbs, the worst cramps I'd ever experienced. Of course, it did, since they hadn't moved in a hundred years.

The liquid drained out, down. Far enough to expose my face. At least the air was warmer than the liquid. I lay still, trying to flex my hands, my feet to encourage movement back into disused muscle.

As soon as I felt I'd be able to do it without hurting myself, I reached up and grabbed the mask from my face and pulled it away. I'm not afraid to say, as much as I'm a gentleman, the first word out of my mouth was a swear word aimed at the weird stabbing pains throughout my body.

Once I'd moved the mask away and the tubes out of my nose, I sat up. This was another exercise in agony and it took far too long. It'll be easy and painless, my ass. I knew we were being lied to all along.

When my airway was clean, I did the one thing I'd been longing to do since I woke. I screamed. Help, over and over again. Help. I'm not saying my poor, abused body screamed it loudly, but I screamed it nonetheless. Nobody came.

Somehow, I pulled myself out of the pod naked and dripping fluid. I grabbed the side of the pod and tried to force myself to my feet, but they fell out from under me, sending me crashing to the floor I tried again and didn't even make it to my knees.

The pain was too much, and it was crowding in again making me dizzy and foggy.

The alarm was still sounding. I groaned, rolled onto my side. I could roll, at least. I curled my arms protectively around my head, pressed my hands over my eyes and gave myself the protection of darkness.

I was cold, trembling as I lay there on the floor. I was sure someone should have been by now. Someone else in the room should be awake, at least. Something was obviously very wrong. Maybe their pods had malfunctioned and right now they were all trying to get out. Maybe, by some twist of fate, I'd been the only one who'd been able to free myself.

I made myself think about that. I made myself think about people stuck in their pods, waiting for me to save them. I used the thought to push myself to my knees. The pain wasn't as bad, but it was still there, bone-deep. The cryo should have perfectly preserved my muscle mass but I still felt wasted.

I crawled down to the bottom of the pod, using a hand on its side to guide me. When I got there, I stopped for a second and let myself breathe. It was hard to concentrate, with the alarm still yelling. I risked cracking an eyelid, but the light was almost instantly too much, my eyes too unused to any brightness. I flailed around the pod until my fingers closed on the soft cotton of my clothing, then I pulled it down onto me. A T-shirt, maybe? I draped it over my head and there, in the muted light, I managed to open my eyes.

I lay there for what felt like forever, aching and blinking against the light, but gradually my eyes adjusted. Eventually, I could lift the T-shirt out of my way and look around. Everything was still too much. My head was pounding, and my stomach was feeling more and more tender by the second.

From this angle, I could see that all the other pods were still sealed. Seven of them in this room.

I forced myself onto my knees, and my traitorous stomach did what I'd thought it might and left me heaving on the floor. Obviously, I hadn't eaten anything, so I just spit up bile and ached, my muscles cramping with the effort of retching.

Honestly, at that point, I could have curled up on the floor and just stayed there. The last thing I wanted to do was to move. But the other pods were there right in my line of sight. Closed. Eileen, my best friend, was in her own pod in another room. She might have been trapped. Anything could have happened to her. It was glaringly obvious something was wrong, and I had to be the one to help.

I crawled across the floor to the first pod and pushed myself up to see the panel mounted on the front, the one monitoring vital signs. I hit the button to activate it.

It lit up, flashed for a second, then settled to show nothing. No heartbeat. No breathing. Nothing.

That couldn't be right. Maybe there'd been a system malfunction. I frowned and pulled myself further up so I was propped on the lid of the thing and had proper access to the panel. We'd all received hours of training on this. It was easy to change the control panel to see the status of the cryo-cycle. According to the pod, this person had been defrosted just like I had. They should have been awake like me.

I climbed down from the pod, then crawled around to the release. It was made big and easy to operate. I released the locks and the pressure, waited with my head between my legs as the fluid gauge counted down, and focused on my breathing.

There was a chime when it was done, just audible over the sirens. I grabbed the handle, released it the rest of the way, and pulled. The lid lifted easily.

Patricia Hammond lay completely still. I reached out and touched her skin and it was cold and damp from the cryo-fluid. But maybe that was normal. She'd just been through the defrost. I'd been so cold when I woke up. Maybe it meant nothing.

I levered myself up so I could touch her, so I could lay my hand on her chest, her neck and search for her pulse.

Nothing.

She was dead.

I yanked my hand back, then fell back onto my ass. She was dead. Patricia was dead. She hadn't been a close friend, more an acquaintance, but we'd worked and trained together, and now she was lying there—dead.

I looked around the room aware of the sirens, the odd absence of anyone else, and the fact I'd been the only one to open my pod. Suddenly, I wanted to throw up for a very different reason. I needed to be out of that room.

I used the pod to push myself to my feet, then stumbled to the door like a newborn lamb, weak and shaking. My own pain was receding in the rush of panic that came over me when I looked at Pat's body. If Pat was dead, and she'd seemed so dead, then why? Was it a general failure or local to her pod? How many other people were actually awake? Where were we? My hands shook and my brain threw me image after image of the ship: alone, drifting through space with only me awake.

The idea of it was almost too big for me to hold. It made my chest ache. Made my heart pound. Made me feel like I might fly apart at any second.

I stumbled through the ship, praying every corner I rounded might bring me to someone else, anyone else. I was still naked. Still coated with the sticky remains of the cryo-fluid. Some part of my brain wanted me to think about what people would think if they saw me like that, but a bigger part didn't care. A bigger part wanted to stumble into Eileen's room and find them opening the pods normally. Find them turning around and laughing at me and my panic. Find Eileen, warm and alive, wrapping me in a towel and holding me.

Every new corner led to another empty corridor. I found the stairwell and screamed up it, but there was no reply so I climbed. It seemed to take forever on uncooperative, shaking limbs, but I did it.

I had to find her. She was my best friend, so I had to find her. Everything would be okay, if only I wasn't alone.

Her floor was two levels up from mine. It was deserted. I stumbled down the corridors, my limbs becoming more sure with every step. I remembered leaving her here only a few hours ago. Hundreds of years ago.

I found the door to her cryo-room and pulled it open.

The pods were all sealed. Still. Coffin-like. Now I noticed, all of them had red lights flashing on their panels. I must have deactivated the one on Pat's panel when I hit it, not even noticing it first. I couldn't remember if the flashing light was normal. I could only stumble across the room until I found the one with Eileen's name carved into a plaque on the front of it.

I fell to my knees beside it, leaned over to touch the screen, and I watched with rapt attention as it flickered to life.

Nothing. No breath. No heartbeat. Nothing.

I bit back on the scream. It was wrong. It had to be wrong. There's been a problem, a miscalculation. There had to be a system malfunction somewhere, and just because Pat was dead it didn't mean everyone was dead. It didn't mean Eileen was dead.

I pulled at the manual release. But this time, I couldn't tear my eyes away as the fluid level dropped. I started yanking at the lid release too early, but it wouldn't move while the pod was still pressurised.

Then, all at once, the lid gave. It slid open, too fast. I wasn't ready.

She was pale. So pale. I reached out to touch her and she was cold. I lay my trembling hand on her chest and there was no movement: no rise and fall. I jerked up and put my hand over her mouth, but there was no telling puff of breath.

I thought about CPR. I thought about the medical room with the defibrillator. But those things were for people who were just slipping into death. People poised on the cusp. Eileen, pale and wasted, was so undeniably gone. Her paper-thin skin was taut over her bones. Suddenly, I couldn't touch her anymore. I pulled back, let the lid fall down, and slammed it fully shut.

If I didn't have to look at her, she wasn't dead. Not really.

A vivid memory flashed into my head. Her hand was holding mine as I sobbed. I explained to her that I needed to back out, they'd never let me in on the mission, and my continued training was useless because what use was a gay man on a colony meant to ensure the survival of the species. The world was falling apart. War, disease, rising sea levels. We were meant to be their only hope, a new start so even if they didn't manage to stop global disaster, there'd be something. Humanity would go on. She'd leaned in, brushed my tears from my cheeks, and told me not to give up. I'd have walked away, but she pushed me. I wouldn't be here if she hadn't pushed me to keep my identity secret, if she hadn't helped me and stayed single to let people presume things about us. To let them think I was straight enough to be worth a place on this mission. No role for gays in the repopulation of the human race.

My stomach rebelled again, and I had to kneel there, retching. I'd cursed them, somehow. Cursed them all. If only I hadn't lied. If only I hadn't made all those jokes about the cryo-pods being coffins. They looked like them and now they were. Hundreds of coffins.

I wondered if anyone else was alive. They had to be. I couldn't be the only one. I couldn't. What were the odds? I probably hadn't heard them, that was all. They were probably weak like me or disorientated. It seemed like it'd taken me so long to wake up.

The pods were meant to be safe. They'd promised us. They'd shown us how it worked so many times. It should have been safe.

I retched again. I sobbed. I lay there on the ground next to the box with Eileen's dead body and I shook.

Chapter Two

I DON'T KNOW how long I lay there, full of pain and fear, but I was still mid-panic when I heard the footsteps. I stopped and sat up, eyes wide, just as they skidded to a halt in front of the door I'd left open. Commander Belka turned and met my eyes.

He had the same kind of naked relief on his face I had in my heart. Someone else was here. I wasn't alone. Thank god, I wasn't alone. At least one more person was alive, maybe others. Maybe there was hope.

He was wide-eyed and pale, though he'd taken the time to dress and seemed surer on his feet than I did. He stumbled a step towards me, then his eyes darted around the room, taking in the pods.

"Dead," he said slowly. "They're all dead."

A sob tore from my throat, apparently the only noise I could make any more, and it pulled his attention back to me. He stumbled a few more steps towards me. I must have looked terrible, but he didn't hesitate before dropping to his knees next to me and reaching for me. I let him touch me, the hands that closed on my arms trembling. I let him pull me forward, let myself be pressed into his arms. He was so solid and warm and so incredibly alive.

I wasn't the only one left. I felt something in me release with just that knowledge. As long as I wasn't the only one. As long as I wasn't alone.

I pressed my face into the coarse material of his uniform jacket and clung to him. I held him close enough I could feel the rise and fall of his breath through his rib cage: the immediate evidence that he was there with me and alive, and I wasn't going to have to face this alone.

We sat there for a while and when he pulled back he looked calmer, more determined. I'd have stayed there longer, clinging to him, but he gently moved me back. He stood and helped me to my feet.

"Crewman Harris, right?"

I could have laughed. Under any other circumstance, I'd be ecstatic that he remembered me. The most important man on the mission knew my name. It seemed too irrelevant now.

"Alex," I said, my voice shaking. "I'm sorry. I'm not..."

"It's fine," he said, smiling softly and squeezing my arm so gently I almost believed it. "Come on, let's get you dressed."

Stood next to Commander Belka, I was aware of my naked body in a way I hadn't been before. He was so tall and broad, and there I was, next to him, completely exposed. I turned, pulling myself out of his hands and grabbing the clothes from the pod next to Eileen's. They were a little too big for me, but the trousers fit well enough not to fall down. I didn't bother with the jacket, so I just pulled on the T-shirt. Unlike Commander Belka, I didn't have the mental energy to dress—not with my body still filthy from the pod.

When I turned back, he was reading the plaque on Eileen's pod giving her name and her date of birth, as if it meant anything to any of us now, so many years and miles away from Earth. As he trailed his finger over the words, I had the sudden irrational desire to push them away and demand he not touch her.

Instead, I cleared my throat audibly. He pulled his hand away and turned to me.

"Your friend?"

"Yes," I said. At that moment, I felt every second of the hundreds of years I'd been in stasis.

We'd met Belka once before, when prepping for launch. Then, he'd been beautiful, all soft, brown skin and gentle eyes. He'd joked with us as we walked past, and I'd felt so pleased with the attention. Eileen had laughed at me afterwards about how I'd fawned and how obvious my crush had been.

I was suddenly glad I'd closed the pod again, and he couldn't see her. She wouldn't have wanted that. I couldn't look at her myself. He frowned and reached up to activate the screen. I couldn't watch and see the lack of a heartbeat again.

He touched my arm, and I stepped back. I didn't want his comfort. He didn't reach for me again.

"We need to assess the situation," he said, voice soft and level. "We need to find out what happened and why. First, though, I want this damn alarm off."

Honestly, in the haze of finding Eileen dead, I'd forgot about it. It'd been a distant worry. Now, once he'd said that, I couldn't stop noticing it again. I nodded, then followed him back out into the corridor. He strode like he was still in charge, as if this was all part of a plan laid out back home, and he just had to follow it through to save us. It was easy to fall in behind him. Easy to let him lead.

The ship had been constructed vaguely like a pyramid, made to sit on its base, which was stocked with supplies. The middle levels contained the cryo-pods and the top levels were reserved for command. Commander Belka lead us to the stairs and he started to climb.

It finally flickered through my mind that the fact we could climb meant there was gravity. It was harder to walk than I'd expected but at that point it was hard to tell if it was a gravity thing or just the tiredness of my limbs.

There was a faint scent in the air, and it could be something wrong with the ship or it could be the scent of our new planet. Either way, we were on a planet. We were somewhere.

I'd never been on the command level before, just a simulation. It was a small, round room. All the computers were wall mounted so they couldn't come loose while in space. All the chairs were bolted down. I turned to look at the back wall, at the familiar quote: "We must accept finite disappointment, but never lose infinite hope." It was a Martin Luther King Jr quote, and I remembered the ceremony when it had been unveiled, selected from thousands of suggestions as a moto to carry us forward, to remind us we carried the hope of a race and that, though the planet we'd left behind was plagued with war and disease and humanity was teetering on the brink of destruction, there was hope. We carried that hope.

I felt the weight of the quote now and turned away from it. I didn't feel much hope.

The front wall was a large display, a real-time projection of everything going on with the ship right now and Belka broke off to head to a panel, probably to stop the alarm, but I kept staring and searching. The ship was still running through defrost cycles, which explained why Belka was more together than me: he'd been awake longer. But there should be more people awake. It shouldn't be just us.

The alarm finally cut out as I went to one of the stations. For a moment, everything seemed so much louder; namely, my footsteps thundering in the sudden quiet. I activated the console and logged in.

It was easy to bring up the cryo-pod monitoring data. There were lines and lines of information, pod numbers, crew names, and the space for vital signs. Each vital sign space the same, o.

No heartbeats.

No breathing.

No life.

Nothing.

My hands were shaking. I knelt down and pushed my head between my knees, as I tried to focus on my breathing I knew was coming too fast again. There was something wrong with the monitoring, there had to be. There was no way they could all be dead, the pods had to be malfunctioning. Only, Eileen's pod hadn't been malfunctioning, she was dead. Pat was dead.

Why wasn't I dead? Why had I survived? I'd been in a room with seven other people who, according to this computer, were dead. It didn't make any sense.

I wanted to scream, and to cry again. Suddenly, I couldn't think of one reason why I shouldn't. It was over. It was all over.

"Alex." Belka sounded worried. He was there, kneeling next to me, and I hadn't even heard him move. "Alex, what happened?"

"They're all dead," I said, gesturing towards the panel.

He frowned, like I couldn't be right. I'd have resented it, if I didn't want so badly to be wrong or to have missed something. To have done something to make the computer tell me everyone was dead.

I must have been right, though, because for a moment he looked desolate. I thought he might sink down there on the floor next to me, and the two of us might lie there and cry together until we just wasted away. But a second later, the expression was gone and he looked confident again.

"Okay, this looks bad. It might be a software malfunction, though, and even if it isn't, we're not the only ship."

"What?"

"Alex," he said, turning to look down at me. He looked so self-assured. So strong. "We're not the only ship. This...this looks terrible. This is a tragedy, and I hope beyond all hope this is a technical malfunction or something, but even if this is true, other ships came first. There were others after. We're not alone. There are probably people heading here to help us right now, and we just have to keep it together, Alex. Can you help me with that?"

I wanted to say no. Wanted to give up and cry. Wanted to point out that, if we'd had this happen, the other might have too. That maybe none of the ships had arrived in a fit state to set up a civilisation, a new Earth.

The thing was, he looked like he'd turn the world over to make what he believed true, and right then, I needed that. I needed belief.

"Okay," I said in a weak voice. "I'll help in any way I can."

"Thanks, Alex," he said, voice and eyes soft. He reached down, took my hand again, and pulled me to my feet. His hands were so sure.

How could I not believe in him?

"I think you need to rest," he said. "It'll feel better when you've rested. We'll have some perspective."

I nodded. I wasn't sure what kind of perspective it'd give me, but I knew I wanted to try. For him, I wanted to try.

Chapter Three

I SLEPT ON the floor of the private room that held his pod—
or I tried to, anyway. I mostly just lay there wishing he was
with me. It felt dangerous to be out of his sight, like he could
have a heart attack or something, and I'd just be there
waiting for him alone forever. I imagined being there alone,
having to carry on alone. I don't think I would have. I think
if he had died that night, I'd never have got up from the floor
again.

By that point, I was convinced everyone was dead. If
they weren't, they'd be defrosted by now. They'd be awake.
We'd have found them in our quest for blankets or heard
them stumbling through the halls.

Belka hadn't accepted it. He was out checking pods
while I lay there, not sleeping. It was probably the
responsible thing, to actually physically make sure what the
computer was telling us was true, but my hands shook when
I thought about it. They were dead and they were
surrounding me. Pressing in on me. Every time I closed my
eyes, I saw Eileen's face. I remembered Eileen's mum, last
time we were together. So proud and scared and brave.
She'd given up her daughter for nothing. There would be no
new Earth for Eileen. No future.

None for me either, probably. But at least I still had a
slim chance. I couldn't believe in it in the bone-deep way
Belka seemed to, but if a ship had made it here, if we weren't
the only ones...

It was something to live for.

I drifted for a while. I must have slept at least a little as I jolted out of a nightmare bad enough to have me screaming, listening for the echo of it in the empty halls.

I wasn't alone. I had to remember that. Not yet.

The temperature rose steadily through the night—presumably our ship acclimatising to the new habitat. The faint scent on the air became more noticeable too. Fruity and rich. The air vents must have come online, which they were set to do once the ship's computer automatically tested the air quality.

We'd not had any instruction on what to do if the air wasn't up to quality. It probably said a lot that we got on the ship anyway.

In the end, I couldn't wait anymore. I crawled out of bed and found my way to Belka's wash room. It was tiny, with a toilet and a shower cubicle, complete with suction devices so they could be used in zero-G for if there'd been a disaster in transit and the commanders had been woken up—as opposed to the plain old disaster we had where they kept on sleeping.

It felt good to shower, felt good to get the scum from the pod off my skin. When I stepped out again, I had to use Belka's discarded towel to dry and put my slacks from the day before back on, but it still felt better.

I edged back out into the room. It felt wrong to leave, like anything might be outside the shut door, and I was only safe here, but I needed clothes. In the end, I scurried down the corridor to the first crew room and swapped out my old slacks for a new pair with a slightly better fit, and a new T-shirt. Then I detoured by the command level and grabbed a tablet computer from a storage locker. Not as powerful as full computer access, but it'd be enough.

Back in Belka's room, I turned on the tablet and booted into the pod systems.

Sometime later, the door opened. I jumped, the tablet falling from my hands and cracking on the floor as cold adrenaline flooded my system. It was Belka, of course. He looked pale, grey, and devastated.

"Alex," he said, and my name sounded like a prayer. He wasn't alone, either, he had me.

"Hi," I said, forcing a smile

He nodded, stepped further into the room, and sank to his knees. I knew then everything I needed to know about how successful his mission had been. I was right: We were alone. I reached out to grip his arm and he lay his hand on mine. For a second we stayed there just breathing, and then he shook his head and pulled back.

"You're up," he said, voice thick. "Did you sleep at all?"

"A little," I lied. "I couldn't sleep in here. Couldn't stop thinking. Too many dead people."

Belka nodded, as though he understood. He must have felt it too, walking those halls. Stumbling from corpse to corpse in the hope of finding something different.

"I've been looking at the data. I'm pretty sure there was a malfunction in the system," I said softly. "It was within a few years of us leaving Earth, I think. As far as I can tell, and the data's sketchy, some kind of interference caused the computers to reboot. That had to be it."

"They starved, I think," he said, voice hollow. "I checked nutrient reserves, and they're much higher than they would be if they'd been sustaining life. I think the system failed. I just... we were lucky."

"They didn't feel any pain," I told him. It felt inane, but I'd told myself that over and over again as I'd combed through the data. I hope he found it more comforting than I did. "They never woke up."

Cryo wasn't perfect. It didn't stop life entirely, it slowed it down though. Like extreme hibernation. They might have lived for decades after the food shut down, but eventually, the body would have run out of its own resources.

For a second, we sat there and absorbed that. It was a fluke that we were here at all. A fluke that our pumps had started up again when nobody else's had. We were lucky. That was all.

I didn't feel lucky.

Belka sat up. He took the tablet out of my hands and set it aside. He reached over and squeezed my arms. He was so warm and alive.

He might be the only person I ever touched for the rest of my life.

Suddenly, the urge to run down to Eileen's pod was strong. The urge to shut myself in there with her, to lie there until I wasted away too. Maybe I could put myself back to sleep. It wouldn't be so bad to drift away in my sleep.

Belka must have seen some of that on my face as he took my chin in his fingers, tilting it to meet his. He looked serious.

"It's going to be okay, Alex. We're not alone on this planet. We just need to get outside the ship and set up the communications array. That's all. You can help me with that, right?"

I wasn't sure I could, but I nodded anyway. He smiled and pulled me forward and hugged me.

I was alive. He was alive. Maybe we were lost for now, but we had each other. Neither of us were alone and, whatever I wanted, I couldn't leave him alone. It would be beyond unfair.

I squeezed him back, hung on. For now, all I had to think about was Belka. I just had to cling to him and survive, and I'd make it through this. Then I could rest.

Chapter Four

ONCE I REALLY started thinking about leaving the ship, I couldn't settle again. There was a world out there, and it was full of things that weren't dead. The ship felt like a mausoleum, echoing with our every step.

I had to wait while Belka washed and changed his clothes. The two of us together went up to the command centre to turn the cryo-pods back on. It wouldn't save anyone, of course. They were all dead. But it'd stop them from rotting. Preserve them. Then, when we found other people, there could be an investigation. We could at least take them out and bury them.

I was very careful to think about it in general terms, not terms specific to Eileen. I could think about Eileen specifically later. When we'd seen the planet. When we at least knew we weren't about to step out into a hostile world where we'd have to fight just to exist.

The lower level of the ship was packed with, supposedly, everything we'd need for our new life here. There were easy to construct temporary dwellings, simple furnishings, all-weather sleeping bags, rudimentary earth moving equipment, some weapons, dehydrated and freeze-dried food supplies; and most importantly, there were seeds. Millions of seeds. Enough to grow any crop we could want, if the soil was good enough. We hadn't been able to bring familiar animals but plants...

Belka led us down between the secured piles of equipment. I trailed uncertainly after him, torn between the fear of what was going to be beyond the spaceship and the need to escape the crushing presence of so much death. My feet scuffed the floor as though reluctant to move. My hands kept brushing against the walls, perhaps hoping a finger would catch and hold me back. But Belka kept going forward, and I kept following him. He was all I had, and I wasn't letting him out of my sight again.

I hadn't been slated as one of the people who'd have their feet on the ground first, but the possibility of a few lost lives on arrival had been addressed, and we'd all been trained for everything.

Still, when we reached the door and Belka moved to check a set of landing gear, like we'd been taught to, I carried right on past him. There was only one window on the ship, and it was small—a porthole, really. It was set into the side of the door, and as soon as I saw it, I needed to look out to this world we'd landed on. Needed to know what kind of place this was, if it was even somewhere we could survive. There was a blind over it, and I reached out before I could stop myself and rolled it up.

Outside, the light was low, the kind of low that probably meant sunrise or sunset. The window was set quite high in the ship so I could see out across the terrain. We were in a forest of some kind. Tree-like plants grew up as far as I could see, rich in shades of green. They didn't look quite like the trees I grew up with, though I couldn't see them in enough detail to be sure. Our descent had scorched the earth for an area around the ship so they were far away, but they were real. Life. We hadn't been sure it'd exist here. We thought the planet would have all the necessary components of life but to see we'd been right, to see alien life for the first time, it was amazing.

The forest stretched for a long way with no sign of habitation, though that didn't have to mean anything. There, in the distance, was a range of mountains, and it was reassuring to see them. Rocks here couldn't be intrinsically different to rocks back home.

Belka cleared his throat behind me, and I jumped.

"Well," he said, smiling softly. "What's the view like?"

"Alive," I said, smiling and stepping back. He stepped forward, putting a hand on my hip to keep me near as he looked out. Maybe he wasn't ready to be alone yet either. Of all the possible worlds, this one looked like it could be made a home.

"We made it," he said, a little awe in his voice, then he turned to me and hugged me again. I let myself relax in his arms, into the reassurance and warmth of him. "I almost didn't believe, but there's really a planet here we might be able to live on. We made it."

"We made it," I echoed, squeezing him tight. "So, let's get out there."

He pulled back with a nod and a laugh that felt almost too sharp and dragged me by my hand to the gear. We both suited up in thick, long-sleeve clothing. It was better to be safe. We even carried backpacks of supplies, in case something terrible happened in the few hundred metres we realistically intended to walk.

Belka finished his kit with a gun strapped to his side. I left mine. I wouldn't shoot anyway. Belka raised his eyebrows when he saw this but didn't comment, just took my elbow and moved me to the door.

"Are you ready?" he asked.

"Yes," I said, excitement bubbling. This was what I'd been dreaming about for years. Not the space travel. Not the saving of our people. This. Stepping out into a new world. Exploring. Seeing something nobody else had ever seen.

There was a sudden stab of guilt, a flash of Eileen, dead in her pod, who'd wanted this, too, and would never have it. Who'd played explorer with me as a child in her back garden, her dad watching us through the curtains and smiling. Eileen, who'd actually turned this dream into a reality for one of us at least.

I pushed the thought back down as well as I could. Later. I'd feel bad later. For now, I reached over and grabbed Belka's hand. He seemed surprised, but before I could second-guess and pull away again, he smiled, squeezed my hand in his, and opened the door.

I'd like to say I sprinted out into the forest, ran through the alien trees, discovered a million species, laughed and smiled, and left all my worries behind me. The truth of it was far more mundane. The door opened to a ladder down the side of the ship, which sloped away like a particularly steep pyramid. We climbed down—Belka first—and that first touch of boot on alien soil was on scorched Earth. The boosters that softened our descent and made it so our equipment could survive the landing, had burnt away the trees for a distance back from the ship. Those boosters sat dormant now lifting the entire ship up off the surface of the planet.

We both walked over to them silently. Belka stopped a way back and assessed, but I went right up to them and lay a hand on one. It was still warm. A testament to how much energy had been used setting us down safely.

And we had been set down safely. The ship had worked. If the cryo-pods hadn't failed....

I shook my head, tried to dislodge the thought, and drew back to Belka's side.

"They're still hot," I said, not sure what else to say.

"They will be," he said, nodding. "We need to release the ramp, then we can unload the communications array. They probably already detected our arrival, but it never hurts to call for help."

I glanced up at the sky like I expected a plane to zoom over any second. Of course, the other settlers wouldn't have planes. They'd have a few vehicles like the ones we had, things that looked more like dune buggies than anything else. Even if they wanted to come to us, looking at the forest around us, it could take them weeks.

But Belka just smiled like everything was fine, then turned to start the release mechanism for the ramp.

"We're getting a shelter out, too, right?" I asked, stepping up behind him. "We're not sleeping in the ship."

"We have to prioritise," he said, sounding every inch the commander he'd been raised to be. "The communications array comes first."

"Okay," I agreed quickly, worrying my lip. "But, just, if there's time, maybe we can get a shelter out? I can't sleep in there. I'm sorry. I can't."

He looked at me oddly, then frowned. He stepped in closer, lifted a hand to my cheek, and gently cupped it. It was so unexpected, so tender, I almost cried. I found myself leaning into the touch a little, resting my cheek on his open palm.

"You look exhausted," he said. There was a hint of reproach in his voice like he thought he should have been informed about my lack of sleep before. It wasn't like I was doing anything to hide it. Or maybe he was mad at himself for not having noticed. Either way, he nodded. "We'll get a shelter out. It might only be basic for now, but we'll get it."

"Thank you," I said, and was surprised when it came out watery. I hadn't intended to cry, but suddenly tears were there, threatening the corners of my eyes. To know he was doing this for me, if it was just him, he might not have bothered for days, maybe not at all, which meant something.

"It's not a problem," he said, stepping back a little. "Got to look after my crew, right? Come on, let's get everything we'll need out here in the open, then we can plan our next step."

Smiling, I let him lead the way.

Chapter Five

GETTING EVERYTHING WE needed from the ship was, as it turned out, not so easy. It took several hours and a lot of swearing before we had the kit to build the shelter and the components for the communications array all spread out on the burnt earth.

I was exhausted. We stopped to eat before we built the shelter. The dry food they'd sent with us wasn't really improved by rehydration, but I was hungry enough to choke it down. It was chalky in my mouth and basically flavourless, but it packed down small. If there had been hundreds of us, we'd have enough of this to survive over a year. As it was, the two of us would have been able to survive our entire lives on it. I lay there on the charred earth very much hoping Belka didn't intend us to spend our entire lives eating it.

It started a conversation, at least, about survival essentials. We had a small supply of water, but years in space had left it with a strange taste that I didn't quite trust, and we'd need more eventually. We agreed it wouldn't be hard to find. As the sun rose, the level of moisture in the air seemed to rise, too, and that, coupled with the abundance of life, had to mean there was water near. I hadn't been out past our camp, but I could see plants, strange and unusual, right at the edge of our clearing, and I was itching to explore.

We spent the bulk of the afternoon putting up the shelter. It was easy in theory, but only having two people made it hard to manoeuvre the pieces. I'd built them a million times in practice, but there'd always been at least four of us per hut.

The good thing, though, was all the work made Belka sweat enough to throw away his T-shirt, and I wasn't sad to see it go. He was a ridiculous specimen of a man with the kind of toned, chiselled body the rest of us could only aspire to. As tired and heartsick as I was, I'd have still very much liked to lick him.

We ate again, reluctantly, then Belka turned to the communications array, spreading out pieces and humming knowingly. I watched him a while, no idea where to even start to help, then turned and went back to the shelter.

The thing we'd constructed was a shell. We'd put up the external walls, of course, and the two interior walls cutting the space into three rooms, but we hadn't moved anything else in and—clearly—I was on my own.

I went for the beds first. I say beds: They were more like metal shelves, but long enough to hold a human. I hauled out two of them, one at a time. The shelters were meant, initially, to hold four people each with two beds stacked like bunk beds, but Belka and I wouldn't need that. The shelves slotted into the wall with a lot of effort and fine balance, but I got them both set up eventually. It was a tiny space, close enough that I'd be able to reach between our beds and touch him. That suited me fine. I wanted him where I knew he was still alive.

In fact, the entire chore of constructing the place took longer than it should have because I couldn't stop myself wandering out to check on him. He was fine—of course— every time I looked. But he always looked up to meet me and smiled, like he was glad to see I was still safe too.

I didn't want to go back into the ship, but, ultimately, that's where all our supplies were, and I didn't want to think of what Belka would think of me if I refused. I kept my visits short, moving quickly, and always stayed down on the lower levels where I could almost pretend I was in any old storeroom. I still hated it, but not so much I couldn't grit my teeth and get it done.

I hauled out two mattresses squashed into ultra-dense rolls and decompressed them before fitting them onto the beds, then I grabbed new bedding. The stuff in the pod room was probably still good, but I didn't want to touch it, and it wasn't like we had to ration it, as we'd expected we would.

I went back to the ship for more clothes, too, though I hadn't assembled the under-the-bed drawers we were meant to stash them in yet. That could wait. There was the plumbing first, then the kitchen. The space hadn't really been meant to hold a kitchen—food was meant to be communal—but I'd fit it into the tiny living space next to what was meant to be the bathroom. It'd be cosy, but we'd be fine.

I wondered, half-heartedly, if I'd be able to convince Belka to help me drag another hut out to connect to ours. It'd give us more space, and who knew how long we'd be here? Through the day both of us kept looking to the horizon but there were no signs of human life.

I thought, privately, that the odds of help coming were low. It was hard not to believe at least a little, though, when Belka obviously believed so much.

I went back into the ship and dragged one of the bathroom kits out of its place. I'd have been able to carry it myself, maybe. I'd have had to open it and take it piece by piece, but I could do it. The thing was, my legs were aching, and my back wasn't too happy with me either, and I just didn't want to start a big job like a bathroom I knew I should, knew I should push on. I certainly didn't want to stumble back into the ship in the dark to go to the toilet, or worse, sleep in there again. But it just seemed like so much.

I sat down heavily and surveyed the box. If Eileen were there, she would have dragged me to my feet and made me do it. She would have laughed at my tiredness and my fear of sleeping inside. She would have helped me, made me feel better.

Missing her was like a punch to the gut, crippling and all-consuming, and for a few minutes, I just had to sit there and breathe through it until it receded.

Then I got up and grabbed the toilet. I was aching, but if I got it installed, at least I'd be able to sleep in the cabin and not in the ship. I couldn't spend another night in there. I just couldn't.

The toilet was heavy to carry, but once I got it to where I needed it, it was easy enough to connect to the frame of the house. Setting it up properly took longer and the light was starting to fade by the time I manoeuvred the sink into position. The shower, I decided, could wait until the morning.

I stood there, stretching and wondering if there was any point in carrying on, when I heard Belka's footsteps. I glanced back and saw his eyes on my shoulders, appreciative.

Oh, that was interesting. I'd heard rumours about him, of course, though I never knew if they were true. Elaine was always quick to tell me which of the men on our expedition were rumoured to be bisexual; I think she wanted to make sure I wasn't giving up on love. I'd never dared to act on any of her information, but I'd hoped, when we were settled and it was too late to send me back, I'd be able to find love. Now, with the way Belka was looking at me...

"Commander Belka, I didn't see you there."

"You're still calling me that?" he asked, raising an eyebrow.

"Well, what else should I call you?"

"My name's Luke, you know." I blushed because I did know his name, and he smiled at me again. He must have been as sore as I was from the day of hard work, but he looked satisfied. Looking at the curve of his lips, I could forget for whole seconds the ship lying dead behind me.

"Luke," I tried. I liked it. "Fine. Are we done for the day?"

"It's getting too dark to work," he said. "I thought we could eat and sleep. Did you get far enough for us to sleep out here or...?"

"Of course, I did," I said quickly. Even if I hadn't really, I'd say I was done enough to not have to stay in the ship. "The shower isn't in and I haven't put in a kitchen yet but..."

"We won't really need a kitchen, will we?" he asked, frowning. "I mean, the nutrient packs only need water added to them. I know you're against going into the ship on principle, but I'd think going back for hot water would be okay. We won't be out here alone for long, after all."

I nodded, though I doubted the truth of what he was saying. Plus, the only hot water was on the occupied floors with the bodies. I wasn't going back up there, if I could avoid it. I'd just do the kitchen the next day when he was busy with something else.

"Good," Luke said, reaching out to squeeze my arm.

We went back into the ship one more time that evening for the lamps and for food. Luke took pity on me and fetched the water then poured it into the pouches of powder before leaving me to stir them into a paste while he set up all the lights. We ate sitting on out beds—since there weren't any chairs yet—and I found myself yawning before it was even completely dark.

Luke didn't make fun of me, just dimmed the lights. I curled up in the sleeping bag on the bed that was apparently mine and let myself drift off to the sound of him humming as he puttered around the tiny space.

Chapter Six

THE NEXT FEW days blurred together in a rush of construction. The first morning there, I tried to help Luke out with the communication array, but it quickly became obvious that he had a system, and it was one I didn't understand. I'd never built one myself, so I couldn't really help, and by the evening, we both agreed it'd be easier for me to focus on other things.

I mainly worked on the shelter. I finished fitting the shower and took out a table and some chairs. Since I wasn't needed for the construction of the communications array, Luke didn't mind me setting up a small kitchen. I thought about asking him to help me extend the shelter a few times, but I couldn't think of a way to do it and justify the two of us still sleeping in the one small room. So, in the end, I kept my mouth shut.

I built the drawers for under the bed and a small set of shelves for our belongings that fit neatly between them. I brought out chairs and then spare sleeping bags to drape over them like blankets. The chairs had been designed more to be easily packable than to be comfortable.

I sorted through the stores we had left. I dug out all the scientific equipment, though Luke raised an eyebrow at me when I did. He didn't seem to like the reminder that we might not only be here for a few days but possibly even weeks.

I watched the ship a lot. I thought about Eileen. Everything I did seemed to remind me of her. Mostly, I wished she'd been spared and not me. If she had been there with Luke, there'd be hope for the species at least. Even if they were the only ones—something my heart accepted more and more as a possibility for Luke and me with every day that passed—they'd be able to have kids. It'd be a ridiculous species bottleneck, but it'd be hope.

If it was only me and Luke, if nobody else ever came, humanity was probably dead. Every time I thought about it, I started to panic and had to busy myself with other things.

Besides, children aside, Eileen deserved it more than me. She'd keep faith in a rescue. She'd help with the communications array. She'd be stronger, braver, and better. She always had been. When we'd decided to do this, it had been mostly her decision. She'd been selected as, well, basically an explorer, while I trained to sit in a lab and look at what she brought back. It had been okay, it had to be. She was just better suited than I was. Luke reminded me of her in a way. Competent, steady. They'd have had amazing species-saving babies.

I spent time watching the forest. Surreptitiously, of course, while I pretended to build something or dig a hole for the waste from our septic tank (and didn't I just get all the fun jobs). It was impossible to just be lazy when Luke was working so hard on the communications array.

At first, I was waiting for someone to emerge. I figured we wouldn't get too much notice if a vehicle or something was going to arrive with the forest being so thick. Then, as the days passed, and hope started to dim, I watched it with intrigue.

I wanted to go into it. I'd been to the edge, touched the plants that looked like trees. Their trunks were much softer—almost like the thick leaves of succulents—to the touch but firmer, less flexible. Something in my heart wanted to dissect one. Wanted to find the creatures here, we'd only seen plants so far though sometimes we heard things. Wanted to go find the water we kept talking about needing. Wanted to explore.

It was dangerous, though, and Luke was always so busy.

The good thing about those days was Luke. It would have been so easy for both of us to sink into despair. To stop caring. To let ourselves waste away in grief. Luke never faltered, though. He smiled and kept going. Kept caring. Kept pushing me to care.

Every day I loved him a little bit more for that.

Chapter Seven

I WOKE WITH a start, heart pounding and breath coming in gasps. Around me the room was dark and still. But then, the bedroom was always dark. Windows weren't a luxury that'd been factored in when they'd designed our tiny shelters. There wasn't even the faint wash of light from this planet's tiny twin moons. Not the light of the stars. Nothing.

I was cold. Too cold. It was warm on the planet. So far, it had seemed almost ideal, but I was cold. It was like the cling of the cryo-pod embedded somehow into my skin. A part of me. Pushing below my surface right down to my bones and sinking into me, a tattoo of sensation.

I had to move.

I got out of the bed slowly, putting my feet over the side of my shelf and letting them lower to the burnt earth below. For a second, I thought it'd be like when I left the pod, that my limbs wouldn't hold me, but I pushed up to my feet, and, somehow, they did. I managed to stand up.

I was close enough now that I could hear Luke's breathing. He was the perfect bunkmate, really. He didn't snore. He didn't sleep talk or sleepwalk, and he was so conscientious of my personal space. Of my needs. I didn't know what I'd done to deserve him.

Part of me wanted to resent him. Wanted to kick him until he was awake too. It wasn't the first time I'd woken in the night, and I doubted it would be the last. It should have infuriated me to know he was there, sleeping. It didn't. It made me feel better. Made me feel comforted.

Absurdly, for a minute, I wanted to reach down and touch him. Wanted to push my way into his bunk, and to curl up in his arms. Wanted the knowledge of his life.

Only, what if he wasn't alive?

What if I touched him and his skin was cold? Cold like the corpses I'd touched in the ship before I hadn't been able to handle it anymore. He obviously wasn't right now, but he could die soon. Or what if I was dead and this entire thing, this ridiculous paradise, was in fact just some ridiculous hallucination. Some dream or half-dream. Maybe I was still in a pod, the ice slowly sinking to the last working parts of my brain, some death surge giving me this one vision of some kind of paradise.

Only, in my paradise, we wouldn't be alone.

I needed to breathe. I stepped back towards the door and let my fingers close around the handle. I wanted to go the other way towards Luke. He probably wouldn't even mind if I'd touched him. He'd be calm. He'd try to convince me help was coming.

I opened the door and stumbled out into the living area. It was tiny, and we combated claustrophobia by leaving the door open, which let the light of the twin moons wash in.

It was warm outside. Of course, it was. It was warm inside. It was only my skin that couldn't understand that. My body.

I leaned back on the wall of the shack, closing my eyes and forcing my hands into fists. You'd think I'd be used to this, to dealing with death. My dad died when I was nine. Old enough to know but not to really understand. To know he was very ill and he was going to die but not old enough to know what death meant. It was only years later that the certainty of it really came home to me. That it meant forever.

That dad would never be anything but a few fading memories.

Eileen would never be anything but a few fading memories.

The thought of it was almost too big to hold. Too immediate, too pressing. It made my knees buckle and my face fall, tore into me and made me press my face down to the burnt ground. She was gone. I was here alone with Luke and he'd been so good and clung so completely to hope, but he could never understand what I'd lost. Even if the other ships were here and humans came crashing through the forest the next day, they'd never be able to replace the cadence of Eileen's laugh or the lives of the other people who'd been on the ship. People I'd learned with and worked with for years.

It felt like a long time before I could stand up. My stomach ached like I'd been sick, though I hadn't. My eyes ached too. I knew they'd be puffy and red. Knew I looked a complete mess.

What did it even matter? Who was even going to judge me?

Since I was on my feet, I made my way towards the ship. It dominated the clearing, looming in glorious counterpoint to the nearest mountain. Maybe we'd been wrong to shape our ships like pyramids, like tombs.

I stood under it for a while, considered going up into it. I could find Eileen, curl up there on the floor next to her, and press my face into the floor. I could give up. It'd be so easy to give up. To just lie there. Easier than walking around and trying to pretend I wasn't dying inside.

I couldn't though. Not with Luke. I couldn't leave him alone.

He wouldn't leave me alone. I couldn't do it to him.

Still, I stood there for a few minutes and I made myself remember, even though the act of remembering felt like a physical pain in my chest. I made myself think of early memories of Eileen—laughing, playing dress up, parading through the house in her mum's high heels. I made myself run down how she'd looked with her dark skin, dark eyes, and infectious smile. The way her eyes had always crinkled when she'd laughed. The way she'd managed to put anyone at ease in a few seconds. How privileged I'd felt to be part of her life. How, when my dad died, she'd not treated me like she suddenly didn't know how to talk to me but carried on like everything was normal. How when I'd come out to her, expecting everything to change, she'd just smiled and held me and told me it didn't matter. We were best friends, and everything was going to be okay.

She'd have made this bearable. She'd have put it all into perspective.

If she was here, I wouldn't have wanted to lie down here in the dirt and give up. It wouldn't have even been an option. She'd make it easy to carry on, to go forward.

"Alex?"

I jumped. My insides rattled. Luke was standing at the edge of the ship, cautiously watching me in the moonlight. I wondered if he could even really see me under here, or if from his perspective I'd be sinking back into the darkness cast by the ship. Maybe that'd be better.

"Alex, are you, I mean... I..."

He'd never not known what to say before. It'd only been a few days, but it felt like he'd turned right to the future, set his eyes on the horizon, and didn't stop. I couldn't do that. I'd never be able to do that.

But, now, he didn't know what to do or say. Somehow, seeing him powerless in the face of my grief made it better.

I took a step towards him, ashamed of how uncertain my legs were. How weak and frail I seemed. He took it as permission and came to me. He met me under the ship and took my hands in his, pressing them to his chest and sighing like he'd found something precious.

"I'm sorry," I found myself saying, surprised at the rawness of my voice. "I didn't mean to wake you up."

"No," he said quickly, squeezing my hands. "You should have. I want you to. I mean, I guess you don't have to. I understand that you might want to be alone, you have every right to grieve however you need to, but, Alex, you don't have to be alone. You can be if you need to, but you don't have to be. I'll be here. I'll be with you. Whenever you need me."

Something in the way he said it made my heart fracture. I pulled my hands out of his and clung to his shirt, my hands bunching the material like that would be enough to force him to stay near and to completely banish the possibility of my being alone.

He put his arms around me and pulled me in close. His arm was warm and heavy around my shoulders and he turned me, guiding me back out and under the starlight. I stumbled but he was sure, firm. He didn't falter, and, with his hands on me, it was easy to focus on going forward. On putting one foot in front of the other.

I gave in to him. I think, then, he could have led me anywhere and I'd have followed. He could have handed me poison and I'd have drunk it. I'd probably have been happy to, actually, but he didn't. Instead, he led me over to his work area, where he'd spread out a tarpaulin to keep his components off the burnt earth. He sat down, pulling me with him. I pressed against him with my face buried in his shoulder.

I cried. Not the nice, gentle kind of crying where a tear hangs daintily from the corner of an eyelash, but big, ugly crying. I sobbed and heaved for breath and clung to him like I might tear chunks out of him if he tried to leave. He didn't. He sat there with me, arms around me, and he was quiet. Quiet and there, taking all my grief and making it okay, making it normal.

We sat there until light started to break into the sky and my eyelids started to feel like lead, and then he stood and guided me to the shelter.

I was glad for the darkness then. Glad to crawl into the sleeping bag laid out on my bed, to let him help me settle. He brought me a glass of water and insisted I drink it and, when I found myself reaching for him, he took my hand and held it. Settled down in his own bed, our joined hands spanned the distance between us.

Then I slept.

Chapter Eight

WHEN I WOKE again, the bedroom door was open and light was already creeping in. I felt terrible, like the time I'd had the flu so bad I'd been bedridden for a week. I'd been young then: little enough mum had brought me soup, smoothed the hair back from my forehead, and kissed me awake.

Nobody was here to take care of me now. Luke was here, but he was busy. He had his array. He had his dream we weren't alone.

Maybe we weren't. But a planet was a big place. New Earth was actually bigger than Earth had been, at least a little. Even if people were out there...

I suddenly, desperately, wanted my mum. It'd been a week since I saw her—from my perspective—though of course it was much longer than that actually, and she was dead now. Even if Earth had survived, somehow, she was gone. Dead from old age. I should be, too, but here I was, a universe away, hurting and wanting nothing more than for my mummy to come to hug me, reassure me that I'd be okay.

I was a grown man. I was more than capable of taking care of myself. It didn't stop me wanting, though.

It would have been the easiest thing to stay hidden in bed. It would have been understandable. I don't think Luke would have stopped me. That was the infuriating thing about him. He was just so kind and accommodating. He just couldn't do enough for you, and I loved that and hated it at the same time.

I knew, though, if I stayed in bed, I would carry on staying in bed. I'd done it before. When things were bad, I'd always wanted to give up, to fold and lie down, to let life wash over me. Eileen had been the one dragging me up before, but she wasn't there.

I was going to have to do it myself.

I stumbled out of the bedroom and into the bathroom, such as it was. I used the toilet, then sat there for a while, head in my hands, just focusing on my breath. It felt like everything in me was pulling me back to bed, but I couldn't go. I wouldn't go.

I forced myself to finish up, then gave myself a bath in the sink. I needed to get the shower running, but it felt impossible just then. It'd take more water than I was willing to carry about, so we'd need a stream, and I hadn't even been outside our burnt clearing.

Still, just the idea of water, of really being clean...

I got a new set of clothes and dressed. In the living area, Luke had left a cup with a paste pouch emptied into it. There was water too. I touched it and it was warm still, which meant Luke had been here recently. Perhaps he'd been checking on me? The thought made me smile.

The food didn't, but I choked it down before finding my shoes. My feet were already dirty when I pushed them into the shoes, but it was okay. I hadn't been fully clean since we landed. We'd need to put down a floor, install a shower and really begin to accept this as home.

I couldn't hope like Luke with no regard for reality. I admired it in him, but I couldn't do it.

It was warm outside. Luke was seated by his components, contemplating them. For a minute I thought about sneaking past him, but he looked up and smiled, and I had to go to him. He stood to meet me, stepped out and reached for me, and that told me as much as anything that I must have scared him the night before. I let his hands find my arms and it was no hardship to let him pull me close for a quick hug.

"Alex," he said, my name a blessing on his lips. "Are you... do you need to rest more? I'd understand if you do. You had a big night. Maybe you should..."

"I'm fine," I said, forcing myself to step away from him. "Really, Luke. I'm fine. It's just...it's a lot, you know?"

"I know," he agreed, glancing up at the ship. He probably didn't, not in the way I did. Not to take away from his grief, but he'd been trained at a central command academy. He could have been assigned to any of the ships leaving Earth. He didn't know the people lying there, not really. He'd lost—of course, he had—but in a way he'd expected. He'd been able to shield his heart against hurt.

And, of course, he had the buffer of not accepting our full situation.

How could I hate him for still hoping, though?

"Anyway, it's good you're up," he said. "I mean, it's probably more mentally healthy than lying around, though if that was what you needed, I'd have supported you. But it's good to be moving. Do you... do you want me to stop for the day and maybe we can do something together? I mean..."

"I'd like that," I said quickly. I really would. I'd like not to be alone. "I've just... there's something on the ship I need to do first."

"Are you sure? I mean..."

"I'm sure," I said. He was going to volunteer to do this or to go with me, and I couldn't let him do that. "I think I need to say goodbye, at least a little. I might be a mess when I come back out but..."

"That'll be fine," Luke said. He reached for me again, touching my arm in a way that felt like reassurance. "I'll be here."

I nodded. He would. He was easy to trust.

It was hard to turn from him and go to the ship, but I made myself. Maybe it would have been better to give myself a few days, but that'd never helped before. If I was going to face the truth head-on, I had to do it quickly.

Luke might be able to run on hope, but I couldn't.

I knew he was watching me as I climbed up into the ship, but I didn't let it stop me. As soon as I was inside, I felt the oppressive quiet of it pressing down into my skin. It made me think in clichés like quiet at the grave. I hurried through the storage floor, where it was more bearable, and up towards the command level.

I hadn't been back here before, where the crew lay. Our ship held about three hundred people. Three hundred corpses now frozen to keep them fresh. It was horribly depressing. They deserved more. Someday, I'd give them more; I promised myself that. Someday, no matter what happened, we'd find a way to bury them before the power failed for good and the pods all defrosted.

I thought, then, about going to Eileen's room. It was probably where Luke expected me to go. It'd be reasonable to go there to say goodbye. But Eileen had never been sentimental. She was the kind who moved forward like Luke. She wouldn't have any patience for me kneeling by her pod and sobbing, and it wouldn't do me any good either. It wasn't what I was there for.

I made my way up, up, right to the command level.

Everything was still active. The computer was running with a map of the planet on the screen, the same one we'd had before we left Earth. It seemed so rudimentary, but then we'd been desperate. We'd all felt mortality pressing down on us, and when they found this planet and knew it was reachable with the best technology we had, it had seemed like a blessing. It had seemed like the kind of gift horse not to be looked in the mouth.

There'd been ten ships. The best Earth could build. There had been a collective effort to fill them with the best technology and the best people. We'd all applied in our early teens or been plucked from our schools for being outstanding: brave or clever or team workers or, more often than not, all three. I remember even when it neared time to go, people looked at us with a mixture of awe and pity. We had this chance, this amazing chance to escape from the mess we'd made of the planet. But what a risk. We couldn't have known this new planet would be like this.

I stopped and traced my fingers over the map. The display made the distances between the ships landing points look short enough that Luke and I could take a nice stroll and be at the Russian ship.

I had to know. Everyone on this ship was gone, but if Luke was right, if there was a chance we might be rescued, I had to know.

The ship was made to be scavenged. Eventually, the crew would disassemble it completely. Some things could never be saved, would be destroyed by the ship, but the wall panels were all made to be reusable. It wasn't too hard to strip one back. There was a tool kit stored in an alcove, and, once the wall segment was out, it wasn't too hard to crawl in there, further, to find the next panel. There were several, each thick and hard to move. It'd have been easier with two of us, but I couldn't do this to Luke—not yet—and there was something cleansing about the strain of it. Perhaps it was the sweat soaking into my clothing or the honest hard work, but it made me feel better.

It made it especially rewarding when I freed the last panel, and a breeze blew in, letting me know I'd made my way through to the outside. I set the panel aside, pushing it among the wires and looking out.

Forest.

Up here, I was well above the tree level. I'd picked the side opposite where Luke was working, though, I suspected he'd heard me remove the panel. I couldn't see him or the mountains, but I could see out. Forest. Green sprawling away into the distance, broken only by the occasional body of water, glinting blue in the sun. That was it.

It was beautiful—beautiful and heartbreaking. I swung my legs out of the ship and sat there letting the breeze blow over me. I looked around and squinted like that could make the view change. I guess I hoped if I wished hard enough, I could make something appear, some hint of other life.

There were still parts of forests on Earth we didn't know about, that hadn't been fully mapped. How would anyone find us here? Why would they even try?

We were alone.

It should have been terrifying, but, in the strangest way, it was freeing. We were alone. This was it. I just had to accept this life here, as this was all I had.

Tears were on my cheeks, but they didn't feel like the ones last night, the ones that had poured out of my grief. Instead, they felt cleansing.

We were alone, but we were alone together. And maybe Luke was right. Maybe people would try to reach us. Maybe there were cities out there or vast sprawling farms. People living and dying, having children, falling in love, falling back out of love, and doing the millions of things that made us human.

They wouldn't be able to reach us though. Not even if they knew we were there. We were on our own.

I put the panels back before I left. Luke probably knew, but there was no point rubbing his face in it if he wasn't ready. I got that most people wouldn't be.

When I got back out, Luke was waiting for me. He took one look at me face and opened his arms and I walked right into them and pressed my face into his shoulder.

This was what I had.

This would be enough.

Chapter Nine

IT WAS A few days later when I woke to the air a little colder than I expected. Not terrible, but colder. I lay in bed a little longer then I might have let myself on any other day and pulled my sheets around me.

Thinking of Luke out there working was what got me moving. He was always working, and it made me feel bad for sitting around. I probably still wasn't up to the kind of productivity level I'd been at before we'd left Earth; the weight of my grief kept hitting me at the oddest times, but the only thing I knew how to do was move forward. So, I kept moving forward. For the first time, I wrapped a uniform jacket around myself on top of my T-shirt. I felt like I might need it.

I boiled some water, stirred up the powder into a paste, and then made my way out of the hut. Luke was already working; though, for once, he wasn't bathed in the early morning sun. The sky, which had been uniformly a beautiful blue since we'd disembarked, was dark and clouded. The promise of rain was good. We needed the water, but Luke was looking at the array parts still spread out across the ground.

I went over to his side and bumped his shoulder. He smiled at me.

"Finally awake?"

"Ha ha." I deadpanned.

Some of the components clustered on the ground looked sensitive, which I thought was a less than ideal design. Surely, they could have assembled it so they were more protected, couldn't they? But then, if things had gone to plan, a group of twenty to thirty trained technicians would have assembled this on week two after we'd established ourselves and already had all our basic shelters in place.

"It looks like rain."

"Yeah." Luke sighed. "Just what we all need, right?"

"It'll be good for the water supplies."

"There is that. We're going to have to pick all this up and take it into the ship though. I can't risk any of it being damaged. I'm not even as far as I should be with it, and if we have any more setbacks..."

"Hey," I said, reaching over and grabbing his elbow. Luke was, I'd learned, the kind of guy who spoke with gestures. The quickest way to get through to him was to touch him. "It's fine. You're doing your best."

"Yes," Luke agreed, though he still didn't seem satisfied. "I just don't want to lose any more time."

I glanced up at the ship. I hadn't spoken to Luke about what I'd seen up there, or what I hadn't seen, and he hadn't asked. He had to know I'd looked. The outside panel coming away would have been loud here in this alien quiet. He hadn't asked, though, and I hadn't volunteered the information. It felt wrong to know that even if Luke got his array working, the only people on this planet were probably so far away they had no chance of reaching us, even if they existed. We could well have been the only ship to land.

Luke obviously wanted to cling to hope though. I wasn't going to disappoint him.

Then I had an idea.

"What about one of the gazebos?"

"The gazebos?"

"Yeah," I said, fishing around in my memory for the official name of the structure I wanted and coming up short. "The long tent thing without the sides. For dining in?"

"Oh, we'll never put it up alone. It was meant for a team," he said, frowning at the pieces of electronics around him.

"We got the shelter up."

"That was only meant to take four people. The structure you're talking about is an eight-person construction at least, preferably ten."

"Then we'll have to be ingenious," I said, smiling. It felt like the first time I'd smiled in days. "And strong. But isn't it better than taking it all inside and getting the components out of order? If we get it up and it does rain, you can carry on working out here under it. It's big enough that it should have a decent dry area, even with the wind. We don't know what the weather on this planet's going to be like. This could be the start of a rainy season. It could be like this for months."

Luke gave a slow, careful nod, as if he was taking it all in. Then, he sighed. "You really think we can build it with just us?"

I wasn't sure, actually, but I said yes anyway. It was enough to get him smiling at me, which had been my main goal all along. Perhaps he was just humouring me, glad to see me suggesting something too. Maybe we could take care of each other's smiles from here on in.

It was easy to find the structure. It was stored as a collection of metal poles and sheets and we carried them out between us, talking as we did. None of the sheets were heavy so much as they were unwieldy, and carrying them alone would have been impossible.

By the time we had them all laid out on the burnt earth, the day was heavier and darker.

"That's not looking good," I said, moving over to stand by Luke. "Maybe we should have gone with your plan?"

"No," he said, laying a firm hand on my back. "You're right, this will be better. We just need to work fast."

I nodded, and we abandoned conversation in preference to focus.

The poles were laid out and bolted together to form two long roof panels. They then had brackets on that let you bolt them together to make a gabled roof, which turned out to be the hard part. Holding the pieces in place and screwing them together at the same time was more difficult than it should have been, but we managed. All the time, the sky grew heavier and darker. I started to doubt this was going to be enough, but no raindrops fell.

The entire structure then had to be raised onto its legs. These were long metal poles, one on each corner and two between them. Getting the first two on was deceptively easy, but by the time the last one was in place, we were both sweating, and I knew I, at least, was going to end up with bruises. The air was heavy and close, and we rushed to move the shelter into place.

It felt like the second we finally had it settled, the heavens opened. Drops of rain rattled against the tin of the roof. We darted under it with me screaming and Luke giggling as we clung to one other, and we turned to watch the sky open around us.

Maybe it should have felt weird to reach for Luke so easily, but the truth was, I'd been reaching for a long time. He was the first one to reach back so consistently, to always be there with open arms when I searched for them. I wondered if it was new for him, too, this ability to be so free with physical affection. Was he like this before on Earth or was it something unique to this new world where everything was a little too quiet and still?

The shelter stood firm. It wasn't ideal. The air was still deeply humid, but it kept the worst of the rain off the components, and I felt myself relax.

"We did it," I said, a note of wonder in my voice.

"We did," Luke agreed. His arm settled around my waist and he squeezed me. "You were right, we could do it."

I laughed, leaning into his side and letting him hug me.

The floor was quickly becoming muddy and sodden, but the components were on a tarpaulin at least. I wiggled away from Luke and went to look at them.

He had the body of the array assembled. It was its guts I could still see.

"I don't understand," I said, kneeling down to pick one up. "Why didn't they send more of this assembled? We could have had it up in days."

"You don't know?"

"Don't know?"

"There were... complications. I mean, I know there was no official word, but I thought you'd know. You might have heard a rumour or something."

Eileen was always the one who'd been on top of the gossip, and the grief at the reminder of her was as fresh as ever. I wondered, distantly, how long it would be before I could remember her without it feeling like someone had reached out and scooped out a handful of my guts.

"I... we didn't hear anything," I managed finally.

Luke must have realised he'd upset me even if he didn't know why because he stepped closer and wrapped his arms around my shoulders. "Do you need me to not talk about this? I don't want to upset you if..."

"No," I said. I guess it didn't actually matter. Whatever had happened on Earth was so far behind us now, but I still wanted to know. I wanted to be Luke's partner in this and to feel he could trust in me and talk to me. "Tell me."

"I mean, I probably shouldn't. This is all classified. When they come to rescue us, this can't be common knowledge."

"I won't tell a soul," I swore, trying not to focus on how there might not be a soul on this planet for me to tell. I wouldn't have anyway. I liked the trust too much. It was heady to be able to share his secrets and burdens.

"The thing was... things were worse than we let the press believe. I mean, you know things were bad, I assume?"

"Of course," I said as I pressed myself closer to him. I didn't like thinking about Earth, about the people I'd left there to die.

"Well, it was worse. We hid the true death toll associated with the last round of flu that took out most of Australia. We hid the nuclear tensions in Asia."

"Not well," I said. "We knew about that."

"Did you know a bomb was actually dropped?"

I froze. I hadn't known. I knew there were threats, sanctions. I didn't think anyone would ever be mad enough to really do it.

"It was a comparatively small device. I mean, any device would be too big. But that one, it was small enough and dropped far enough away that we could cover it up. The media'd been falling to pieces anyway. And we just... we didn't know. It was only a test drop, a warning, and tens of thousands of people died."

"And you call that a small device?"

"Alex, a large device would be millions. We were thinking about nuclear apocalypse. We should have waited longer to launch the ships. Things weren't really ready.

Maybe, if we'd waited, we'd have spotted whatever fault made this ship fail like this. But all we were thinking was every day we delayed was a day closer to the end of the world. A day more with the possibility we'd wake up to a bomb falling."

"So... we weren't ready?" I said, reaching out to touch a component. "But we were on time? The ship left when we'd been told it was meant to."

"Projects never run on time," Luke said, and he was still smiling, always smiling, but this time there was a sadness to it. "I'm sorry, Alex. If we'd been thinking, we'd have delayed. This might not have happened."

He gestured, taking in the ship and the dead. I thought about them all lying there, everyone I'd been close to for years including my best friend, who meant more to me than anyone else in the world. They hadn't had to die. They could have survived, if only we'd been smarter. If only the world hadn't been falling apart around our ears. If only we'd waited.

"You don't know that," I said. "Maybe you were right to rush. Maybe, if you'd stayed, we'd all be dead."

"So, I maybe saved one person?"

"Two. We're both here, Luke. We're not alone. It's terrible, but we're not alone."

He nodded, seeming to take it in. He pulled me closer and I went, resting my head on his shoulder and wrapping my arms around him. He was here. I'd lost so much but Luke was here with me: helping me and caring for me. I wasn't alone. I had him and he had me.

"I'll get this thing running," he said softly. "I'll find people. I know it won't be easy, but we can't be the only ones here."

"I believe you," I lied. It might have been better to say I wanted to believe him.

Chapter Ten

EVENTUALLY, WE LET go of each other. We moved to sit at the edge of the dry patch to watch the droplets of rain falling. Once we were settled, Luke took my hand and I shifted closer, close enough to lean on his shoulder and feel the rising and falling of his chest as he breathed. It was soothing. I wondered, absently, what it'd be like to fall asleep in his arms with the certainty of his life right there under my cheek.

Sitting there watching the rain, I was glad to have him. Of all the people on the ship, well, I'd have picked Eileen, but he wasn't a bad runner-up. He was patient, kind, and friendly. I suspected the avoidance thing he had going on wasn't entirely healthy, but I couldn't exactly say I was in the best place mentally. He made it easy to just follow him.

I could definitely do worse.

After a while, we began to talk. Luke told me about how he was enrolled in the programme when he was eight. He'd been orphaned before he was one, but he'd always lived with his grandma, who was warm and kind. She'd wanted a bright future for him, and when the programme had shown interest, he'd grabbed it with both hands. He'd always put everything into it.

He listened to me talk about my mum, York, and our flat. About the summer when I was seven years old and Dad, Eileen and I had built a tree house in the local park, abandoned even before the worst of the damage to the ozone layer drove everyone inside. It was one of the last clear memories I had of my dad doing something with me before he wasn't well enough, though, he'd maybe supervised more than helped. It felt good to talk about him, though it hurt. Now, it felt almost hopeful, like someday I might be able to talk about everyone else and have it just hurt a little but mostly feel good.

He listened to me and stroked my back, and it all felt a bit smaller and more manageable, somehow. Eileen was gone and that was always going to hurt, but for the first time it only felt like it might crush me, not like it was actively crushing me.

I'd take what I could get.

We ran back to the hut during a break in the rain, hands clasped together and mud splashing. I made him stop in the living area, turning on the lights I'd installed earlier so I could really see him.

"Come on, boots off. You're not trailing that mess into the bedroom."

"Alex, we don't even have a real floor."

"Not my problem," I said, bumping his shoulder. Somehow, in the rain with the strange intimacy sitting there talking had brought us, I felt lighter than I had in, well, a very long time. "It's the only home we've got for now, and I don't want you trailing mud all over it."

"I don't see the point," he said, but he sat down and started unlacing his boots. I followed, sitting across from him. It felt good. I didn't even mind when the rain started again, heavy against the roof. At least my water barrel would be full for a while.

"I might have a shower," I said, standing with a stretch. "I mean, at least the water'll be replenished quickly if I do it now." Though I'd installed the unit, the amount of water it took to get a decent shower was really too much for our little setup.

"We did work up a sweat moving the shelter," Luke said, stretching. "And, I mean, what else are we going to do while we wait for the rain to stop?"

I glanced over at him. Luke wasn't looking at me. He probably hadn't meant it in anything but an innocent way, but the words sent ideas rattling around my head that made me blush. Ideas involving the pressing of his skin to mine, or his lips all over me. It felt almost sacrilegious to think about it with the ship right there, but I was only human, and I felt so close to him.

His eyes caught my blush. I watched as they dipped to my lips and a look of understanding settled over him, followed quickly by contemplation. Oh, goodness, he hadn't even thought of it before. He probably wasn't even interested in me.

He stood, broad shoulders flexing, and came around the table. He leaned down and placed his hand on my shoulder, and then moved it to my chin. He gently tilted my head up so he could look at me.

"What do you think, Alex?" he asked, voice suddenly lower. "Can you think of anything else we could do to pass the time?"

I could.

He beat me to action, leaning down to kiss me. All I could do was arch up into him, lifting my fingers to tangle in his hair as I pulled him closer to me and opened my mouth for him to do whatever the hell he wanted.

What he wanted, apparently, was to kiss me deeply and thoroughly. I let him. I couldn't have done anything but let him. I was completely weak when it came to that man.

He pulled back after what felt like both forever and not long enough, pressing gentle, exploratory kisses to my lips, cheeks, and eyelids. I opened my eyes and he was a vision above me, all rumpled and looking so pleased with himself. I wanted to ruin him.

"Hey," I said, bringing my hands up to cup his cheeks. I ran my thumb out to trace the edge of his smile and he looked at me intensely. "Have you done this with a guy before?"

"Yes," he said. "I've been with men and women back on Earth. I'm bi. I'm not only doing this because you're the only person here, Alex. I wouldn't do that to you."

"I never thought you would," I said, leaning in to press another gentle kiss to his lips in hopes the gesture hid the fact that maybe, for half a second, I had thought that. He was just so wonderful. What could he possibly want with me? I trusted him though. If he said this was more than just convenience, I believed him.

I pulled back and he was looking at me like I was his world, like nothing else mattered to him. My heart leaped.

"Let's go to the bedroom," I found myself saying, and it was more than I'd ever felt brave enough to say before.

"Yes," he said into my ear, breathless and needy. "Let's."

He grinned, face splitting in joy, and grabbed my hand.

The cabin being so small meant it was only a short stumble to the bedroom. He kept his hands on my hips as we moved, then held us up in the doorway and pushed me back against the doorframe to kiss me again. I was more than glad to go along with it. More than glad to push our bodies together and gasp as he bit my neck.

I'd always had the impression he was much taller than me, but up close like this, we were more similar than I'd realised. He just gave the impression of being larger than life. Actually, I only had to tilt my head a little to let him kiss me. I only had to stretch to wrap my arms around his broad shoulders.

"God," he gasped, fingers digging into the flesh of my hips. "You're amazing, Alex."

"I'm not," I said, flushing a little. "I mean, just look at you. I'm not."

"Shut up," he said, leaning in to kiss me so I had no choice but to do what he said. "Alex, you're beautiful. I've been thinking... but I wasn't sure you wanted anything. I mean, this is such a weird situation, us being the only ones here. You know you don't have to do this, right? You know, if you're not into men..."

"Idiot," I said, pulling him in for another kiss. I felt his dick hardening through the material of his trousers. "Please, Luke. Let me touch you."

"Always," he said, pushing me back harder against the doorframe. His hands slid around from my hips to my ass and pulled me up to move me so my cock brushed against the v of his hips and, god, that was hot. I loved how he could manhandle me.

And since I'd been given permission, I touched. Hesitantly at first, running my hands up his arms and along his shoulders as he kneaded my ass. I'd spent so long staring at those shoulders; they felt amazing under my hands. My fingers trailed down his spine and grabbed his hips, then they dipped down to cup his ass. The gasp he made tasted sweet on my lips.

"Yeah," he said. "Like that."

"Like this?" I asked, squeezing.

Luke laughed. His ass was just as good as his shoulders: ample and firm.

"Yeah," he breathed. "Like that. Come on, let's get this

onto a bed."

I didn't argue, stepping forward when he moved back so I could stay right in his space. He let me, walking backwards until he sat on his own bunk and pulled me forward, guiding me so I was kneeling over his lap.

I liked the power the position gave me, though it effectively meant I couldn't get at his ass anymore. I just changed my focus, running my hands up under his shirt and over his stomach. It was so hard. I'd looked at it so many times while he was out there working. I wanted to touch it. I desperately wanted to bite him all over and mark him, so, even if this was a one-time thing he regretted in the morning, I'd know it had been real.

I didn't though. I wasn't stupid. Instead, I slid my hands down to his cock, touching him through his pants. He was hard already, and I liked the feel of him through the cotton. I wanted to jerk him off or suck him. I wanted him to rut against me until he came all over me and I could lose myself in him for a little while. I wanted him so badly.

"Alex," he said, voice high. "Come on, open my pants. I said you can touch."

"Maybe I don't want to yet," I said, faking a pout.

For a second, he looked like he was trying to work out if I was joking or not, until I pulled down the zip of his pants and he grinned.

He shifted a little as I reached down and freed him. I wasn't exactly a dick connoisseur but this felt like a good dick to me. It wasn't too long or thick but was just right in the palm of my hand. I curled my fingers around it and stroked gently, so softly that Luke whined. I loved that sound from him.

"Alex," he gasped, my name on his lips like a prayer. "Come on, please. Don't tease me."

"Okay," I said, tightening my grip a little. Pre-come was

beading at his tip and I hesitated a second. "Condoms?"

"On the ship," Luke said. For a second, we both paused. We weren't going out into the rain, but I wanted this. If we stopped now, we might not get back here again, and I needed him. I needed to stop feeling bad, even if it was only for a while. "We were both tested just before we left, and we were clean, or we wouldn't be here."

"That's true. I mean... should we?"

"Please," he said, his voice deep. "I need you."

That was enough. With my fingers, I scooped up the pre-come and rubbed it down his length. This would be better with lube. I hadn't brought any over to the shelter, though. There was some on the ship but the rain was still pattering on my roof...

Of course, I didn't have to use my hand.

"Stand up," I said, climbing out of his lap.

He groaned but did what I said, standing and letting me shove his pants right down. He stepped out of them then, and with a little encouragement, took off his T-shirt too. He pulled at the hem of mine, and I hesitated before letting him pull it up and away. I wasn't as muscular as he was, but he didn't seem to mind, if the way his hands moved over my body was any indication.

"Look at you," he said, all intense. "It's a good job you haven't been walking around with your shirt off. I wouldn't have got anything done."

"Well, what do you think you were doing to me?"

"Fair," he said, leaning in to kiss my neck, distracting me while he reached around and unfastened my pants. I'd been expecting it really, so I obliged when he pushed them and my underwear down over my hips. I quickly stepped out of them and kicked them away.

Then, without any warning, he used his hands on my

hips to push me down onto my bunk. He smirked at me then ran his hands down my side, resting on my thighs. I spread them at his gentle touch and then he sank down between my legs and took my dick into his mouth.

I gasped, hands scrabbling for purchase in the sheets. It was so fast and intense and so very good. He took me as deep as he could, then pulled back just holding me there in his mouth for a second before pulling off and looking up at me.

"Is this okay, Alex?"

"I... yes, of course. I thought you'd want to come first?"

"No," he said, smiling one of those devastatingly handsome smiles again. "I'm going to get you off so good, you're not going to know what's hit you."

I swallowed hard.

Luke went back to what he'd been doing as he took my cock into his mouth and bobbed his head and ran his tongue along the underside. He lifted a hand to cup my balls, then he used it to cover the rest of the length of my cock. The sensation of it was unreal, overwhelming. It wasn't that nobody had ever sucked my cock before, it was just that normally they expected me to do it first and then, when it was my turn, it was over too quickly. Not that the rush was entirely their fault, a bunkhouse in a training facility didn't provide a lot of privacy, so there was always the looming fear someone could walk in at any moment.

Luke took his time. He varied his speed and his rhythm. He tried different things with his tongue, swallowing and sucking around me. It was filthy, but so, so good.

I tried to say something, but I'd never been good at dirty talk. Somehow, even in the most intense moments, the words sounded wrong, awkward. Instead, I clutched at my sheets and I moaned for him, letting my body do the talking. It was so much easier to throw myself back and let myself get lost in the wetness of his mouth.

He pulled off after a while and helped me to turn and lie down. He climbed up over me on the bed, reaching down between us to cup my balls again. Then, he kissed me long and deep.

"You're amazing like this," he said against my lips, though all I was doing was lying there needing him. "Let's just quit everything else we have to do and fuck all day."

"Luke..." I groaned. I wasn't sure where I was going with it, but he seemed to know, because he reached down and took hold of my dick, stroking it gently, then harder. I was already so hard, so close. It didn't take much before I was coming, legs shaking as I spilled across my stomach and cried out against his lips.

We lay there for a while after, me panting and him smirking. I finally convinced my hands to uncurl from the bed sheets so I could reach up to cup his face, pull him down to me, and kiss him. He went happily, bracketing me in and holding me there.

"I didn't think you'd be so quiet," he said after a while. "You're not normally so quiet."

"I... I get weird about dirty talk," I admitted, flushing. "Sorry if you like it. I just...it always feels weird for me."

"Will it bother you if I do it?"

"I don't think so?"

"Good," he said. He moved his hips a little and I could feel him, hard and needy against me. "Because I'm going to tell you just how good it feels to rub off on you, okay?"

"Yes," I said, voice a little too high.

Then, to his credit, he started doing exactly what he'd said he was going to do. He rubbed against my hips, groaning and spilling the filthiest things from his mouth. He told me how hot I was. He went into detail on all the things he wanted to do to me and how good I felt pressed against him. He'd apparently particularly liked the feeling of my cock on his tongue and had ideas about how my mouth would feel on him. I closed my eyes and offered myself up to him, letting myself believe, for a moment, everything he was saying about me was true.

When he came, I leaned over to kiss him. I held him through it, then rolled us both onto our sides to face one another. He was beautiful when he came. I promised myself, if he let us do this again, I'd see that face with my mouth on his dick.

"Hey," I said when he seemed to have come back down to New Earth. "I take it that was good for you."

"Fantastic, sweetheart," he said, leaning in to kiss my cheek. I blushed at the pet name, at the intimacy. "Good for you too?"

"Amazing. But I do think we should take that shower now."

He laughed, then he kissed me one last time, long and deep, before he climbed out of my bed and headed to the washroom. I lay there for a minute, listening to the sound of the rain on the thin metal roof.

Part of me couldn't believe what had happened, the other part thought it seemed inevitable. Either way, I knew not to put too much hope in it. He talked like it wasn't just a one-time thing, but people say a lot of things when someone is touching their dick.

I washed after him, enjoying the fact that the water was plentiful for once. I vowed to set up a few more barrels before the rain came again. I could find the water treatment kit in the ship, too, and maybe now I could go looking for a stream.

When I got back to the room, the lights were dim but

Luke was sat in bed, reading. He smiled at me and held out his hand. I went to him and he didn't take my hand but raised his hand to my cheek and pulled me down for a soft kiss. It was nice. Sweet.

"I wish you could sleep over here with me," he said with a look of disappointment on his face. "But there's no space. I made your bed though."

"It's okay," I said and pulled back. I didn't even have to take a step to be at my own bed and he had remade it. A new sleeping bag, even. He must have taken them from the drawer under the bed. I didn't even know he knew I kept them there, though, of course, he must have looked before when looking for clean clothes.

As I slid into the sleeping bag, he slid down too, putting the book away. It felt strange to lie there in the half-light, looking at each other and knowing what we'd done. Strange and lovely.

"Goodnight, Alex," he said softly across the gap, reaching out to turn off the light.

"Goodnight, Luke," I whispered.

I lay there for a moment just listening. It was quiet again. We were still alone. Slowly and uncertainly, I reached my hand out into the space between our beds. It was silly, of course. He wouldn't see it. He wouldn't even know I was reaching for him but...

His hand met mine, already reaching out, like he'd known I'd need him. He laced our fingers together and squeezed. A smile fought its way onto my lips.

For the first time, I believed someday things might actually be okay.

Chapter Eleven

THE NEXT MORNING, I woke up alone like I had every morning. Luke was an early riser, which wasn't going to change just because he had come all over me, but I was still disappointed when I looked over to the empty bed. A little slither of doubt about how I should act settled in my stomach and I hated it. Were we boyfriends now? Was this a real thing, or something that was going to disappear if anyone actually found us? Did it even matter?

I turned over and rolled myself up in my sleeping bag, then rolled back and forced myself out of bed. Lying there feeling sorry for myself was appealing, but it wasn't going to fix anything.

I washed, got changed, made my bed, and ate a pouch of chalky paste. I'd hoped I'd get used to the stuff and start liking it but, if anything, it was getting worse. The thought of eating it for the rest of my life was just intolerable, but I choked it down anyway.

I'd have done some seriously morally dubious stuff for a bacon sandwich.

The shelter didn't have windows, so I didn't get to see the world until I opened the door. It was warm again. The absence of raindrops on the roof let me know the rain had stopped but the ground was still sodden and, for the first time, there was noise.

Opening the door was like turning on a radio. There were creatures in the forest, and the rain had apparently woken them up. It sounded like they were singing for joy. I couldn't help but grin as I stepped out of the door, striking out right away to the edge of the clearing.

It was louder there, almost overwhelming, and I crouched down at the edge of the burnt patch. There were already the tiniest green plants beginning to encroach, which was good to see. The land would reclaim the damage we'd left.

Then I saw it.

It was tiny. I guess if I had to compare it to something I knew I'd pick a beetle but, at the same time, it wasn't quite like anything I'd ever seen before.

It scuttled through the leaf litter and I leaned over to get a better look. Its carapace was a dark green, like the trees, and it had shiny gossamer wings. It seemed to be built in a circle, divided into thirds with each third having an eye and two needle-like legs. It was beautiful.

My fingers itched for a notebook to record it. I wouldn't capture and measure it, I wouldn't want to risk damaging it. Not until I was sure there were others, but there had to be others. The forest had to be full of life.

I wanted to explore it.

"Alex!"

I started back and almost fell on my ass but caught myself just in time. Luke was striding over, already shirtless and sweaty, and I couldn't help but let my eyes trail down his torso.

I'd been able to touch that last night. I might be able to touch it again. He might let me.

I hoped he let me.

"I didn't see you come out," he said, dropping down to kneel next to me. "Have you found something?"

"A beetle," I said, but when I looked back it was gone. "Not too exciting, maybe, but I haven't seen anything alive before. They don't seem to come out to the burnt part."

"I don't blame them," Luke said. He shoved up again and offered me his hand, which I took. He didn't let go when I pulled myself to my feet but used the hand to pull me in, his other hand coming to rest on my back, while he gave me a soft and tender kiss.

At least that answered one question...it hadn't been a one-time thing.

He looked pleased with himself when he pulled back, and I wasn't going to begrudge him that. I smiled down at the ground instead, a blush on my cheeks. It was so nice, so sweet. I wanted him to keep kissing me like that forever.

"So," he said, turning back to the burnt-out area. I followed his gaze and let my eyes fall, for the first time that day, on the ship. My heart sank like it did every time I looked at it. It stood there, dominating the forest and making everything else look tiny and insignificant. Its very presence was dark and rude and full of death.

Full of my dead friends, more specifically. Not only Eileen—though, of course, Eileen—but most of the people I'd known since I was a kid. My first crush was lying dead in there. My first kiss. My first real boyfriend.

I really wanted to not be looking at it. I knew it was never going to stop hurting—the loss—but that didn't mean I had to look up at the thing every day of my life.

"I was thinking," I said, pressing in closer to Luke. "Now might be a good day to go find water in the forest."

"Why?" Luke asked, a rare frown creasing his forehead. "I mean, we have loads of water."

"I know," I said, trying to pick my words carefully. "But..." I really had no excuse other than I wanted to. Other than it seemed an alive and bright place and better than sitting here with our towering box of dead people. "I just think we need to tackle it as soon as possible and why not today?"

"I guess," Luke said, frowning. "But, Alex, I need to work on the array. We need that. You can't go alone."

"I can," I said quickly. "I'll take a rope."

"A rope?"

"There are some in the ship, for exploring." Eileen had used them, I knew. I'd helped her go over her training material so I knew some of the theoretical side of heading out there alone, even if I didn't have her physical prowess. "They clip to your belt and unspool as you walk so you can find your way back. I won't get lost."

Luke looked out at the forest, unconvinced. "What if you get hurt?"

"I won't go far. There might be a stream just a few metres in, for all we know."

"We'd hear it."

"A few hundred metres, then. And if I do get hurt, you can follow the rope to find me. I just think it's important to do this." He looked at me, at the forest, and then back at the ship. I could see him calculating, weighing it up. He'd have to be an idiot to not know I wanted this, and I knew he wasn't an idiot. He evaluated then sighed.

"Don't go far," he said, patting my shoulder. "Scream if something goes wrong."

"Yes, sir," I said, grinning. He rolled his eyes but also didn't stop me as I went to the ship and disappeared inside.

Going into the ship wasn't so bad when I was only there for a short time. I found one of the ropes easily, attaching it around my middle. I almost preferred not to have it, but I saw Luke's point. If I did wander out there and get lost, I wouldn't be able to find my way back. The rope would also remove the temptation to break my promise and go further in. I was limited.

I did stop long enough to grab a couple of water barrels and roll them out of the ship. They were light enough to manoeuvre easily, and I rolled them over to behind the house and stood them on their bottoms. It didn't look like it was going to rain again today but, if it did, I'd be ready.

I glanced back over at Luke as he poured over his pieces and gingerly held something with a circuit board strapped to its outside, then back to the forest. I was doing the right thing. I'd feel better after a walk.

Before now, I hadn't even stepped out of the burnt ash of our landing, perhaps a little afraid that, if I did, I'd just walk away and not come back. But as I did, what I'd taken for grass crunched unexpectedly under my feet. I reached down to snag a piece noticed it had brittle structures inside it, like twigs running up it and giving it rigidity.

I dropped the leaf and made my way to the nearest tree, or what I'd been referring to as a tree. It wasn't, of course. It had a thick, dark-green trunk, but it seemed to be composed mostly of leaves that spread out at the top like the crown of a pineapple. I reached out and touched it, felt its thick flesh. It was like a succulent. I pulled at it and it resisted, only a bit more flexible than I'd expect from wood.

I wondered if it had the same rigid structures inside it and if we could use them to build. That'd been the plan, after all. Find local materials to build with. We hadn't been able to bring enough from earth, I supposed we could theoretically slap a load of shelters together or use panels of the ship to build. The shelters were so small, and I hated the lack of windows.

A little cabin...that sounded a lot nicer. There had to be something on this planet we could make one from.

I pulled myself back. It was better not to think that far ahead when everything still felt so uncertain. I didn't have to colonise the entire planet myself today. I just had to find water.

I looped the rope around the tree and clipped it to itself. I called it rope but it was more like a thin, tough wire. I gave a gentle pull and it held.

I risked one more glance back at Luke. He was working and didn't look up at me. Then I went into the forest.

The trees didn't make up a canopy like I was used to, so there was more light available within the forest. The stems hid a lot, and I hadn't gone far before I lost sight of the ship. I felt like, for the first time since we'd landed, I could breathe.

That day, I spent hours exploring the forest.

We'd seen flashes of colour from our campsite, but it didn't compare to what I saw once I really broke through the tree line and pushed further back from the damage. The entire place was a riot of rich blues, reds and so many purples. It felt almost lavish. There were so many structures reminding me of flowers, but, instead of petals, most of them had a single, petal-like tube, often decorated with swirls or spots.

Under the canopy, there were insects. So many insects. I saw lots of flying ones, as they dipped into the flower-tubes. Long, thin things—perhaps like stick insects, but with the colouring of dragonflies—crawling along surfaces, then suddenly taking flight and manoeuvring themselves down the tubes before emerging.

I couldn't help but wonder if they were pollinating. If they were pollinating, there might be fruit.

And, sure enough, when I looked, I found fruit. It wasn't in the trees, like I expected. It was hanging down low beneath the bushes. Hidden close to the ground were soft, green berries and when I crawled under another bush I found ones with yellow and blue stripes. I'd have ignored them on Earth, taking the colours as a sign of poison, but who knew on New Earth? I took off my shirt and wrapped handfuls of them in it. I could investigate later.

I found myself eyeing up a few of the low plants, wondering if they had underground tubers we'd be able to eat. We had Earth plants to plant, yes. But I couldn't help but wonder about the life that was already here and if they'd provide the nutrients we needed to live.

After a while, I found the stream. It wasn't as big as I'd hoped, but it looked clean and fresh. There were more of the plants with berries closer to the water, and it was the first place I saw a non-insect living thing. It squatted in the mud at the bank, long, fat, and luxuriating. It was bright red in colour and obviously unafraid of being spotted. It didn't even move when it saw me, and I wondered if it was the top of the food chain here. It reminded me of a frog in the face, though more like a lizard in the body. It was neither, obviously. I wanted to touch it, to feel its skin, but I held myself back. I wouldn't want to hurt it.

Instead, I collected a small bottle of water, stashed it in the pouch I'd made from my shirt along with the berries, and turned to follow my rope back to camp.

Chapter Twelve

WHEN I STUMBLED out of the forest, Luke was sitting in front of the shelter eating one of the nutrient pouches. He looked about as enthusiastic as I felt.

"Hey," I called. I moved a step forward, then stopped to unfasten the rope from around my waist. It was easier than unhooking it from the tree. Luke waved and I took my shirt over to him, grinning. We'd set up another table and chairs outside the shelter in addition to the one inside so we could eat lunch there. I took the chance to dump my shirt on the table, letting it fall open and the fruit inside spill out.

Luke raised an eyebrow.

"I found it," I said, smiling. "In the forest. I found the river too. It's a bit of a walk, but it's not so bad. It took me so long because, well, there's so much to see in there!"

"I bet," Luke said, but there was something tight about his smile. "You're not going to eat those, are you?"

"Do you think I'm stupid?"

His eyes widened, mouth opened a little. "What, no! I wouldn't."

"It's fine," I said, dropping into the chair across from him. "I want to study them, Luke. We have some assays for common poisons on the ship, though, I doubt it'll do much. I was thinking of defrosting some of the tissue culture we have and doing a test with that. Definitely some microscopy."

"So, you *are* thinking of eating them?"

I kind of was. "I mean, if they're safe there's no reason not to."

"I guess," Luke said, looking at the berries uncertainly. "I just...do we need to do this? We'll be found soon. They've probably already got working farms. We have crops. We could plant something..."

I glanced back at the ship but quickly looked away again. We could. There were plenty of seeds in there.

I just didn't want to.

"I'm just curious," I lied. "It's an entire new planet, all this life. I just want to see if it's anything like us. And I'm not much use to you with the array."

"There is that," he agreed. "I mean, fine. I don't think we should eat them, but investigating them can't hurt."

"No, it can't," I agreed, then went into the shelter to make up a nutrient pouch. I washed my hands thoroughly first, but it was even harder to choke down than normal with fruit on the table. I wasn't crazy enough to eat any of it without extensive tests, but I could dream.

Testing meant going back into the ship, which I didn't want to do, but there was a small lab set up and it didn't make sense to cart things out into the sun when moving them risked upsetting the calibration of instruments. I sucked it up like an adult and got on with it. Most of my afternoon was taken up with testing the water to see if it was actually drinkable. We'd been using the rainwater to wash but there was a difference in actually consuming it.

It was turning dark by the time I left the ship. Things were looking good thus far, but I knew better than to be lax. There might have been things in the water I couldn't even think to look for though. Frankly, if the water wasn't drinkable, we were dead men walking anyway, so we'd probably just have to run it through the filter we'd brought and hope for the best.

I found Luke back in the cabin. He was boiling up some of our Earth water for a nutrient pack and, when he saw me, added another cup of water to the pan.

"Thanks," I acknowledged, dodging around him to sit on one of the chairs.

"No problem," he said. "How are the tests coming?"

"Water's looking good. I mean, we'll want to put it through a filter but..."

"That's good," Luke said, smiling softly. "This stuff tastes kind of weird, right? From the ship. It can't be helping with the flavour of the nutrient packets."

"No, it can't," I agreed. "If the water's looking good, I think it's close enough that we could take out the small portable pumping station and run a line back to the house."

Luke hummed, looking down at his boiling water. "Not much point, though, really. I mean, we're going to be out of here soon."

"We don't know that," I said softly. "I mean, I hope we are too but..."

But there might not be anyone out there to help us. We both knew that. Luke just obviously wasn't in a place yet where he could say it, and I got that. We didn't exactly talk about the ship either and what we were going to do with it. Sometimes not talking about the thing was the right way to go...

"I mean, either way, it might be a while. And if we get the pump going, there might be some actual water pressure for the shower."

"I won't argue with that being a good thing," Luke said, relaxing a little as I let it slide. "Maybe, after I get the array going."

"The pump by itself is small. I can carry it alone."

"You can," Luke agreed. "Doesn't mean you should."

I rolled my eyes, but there was time to talk Luke around. Also, just because he was technically commander didn't actually mean I had to listen to everything he said. Not now, when there wasn't anyone else to back up his authority.

"How's the array going?" I asked instead, and he was happy enough to chat about some of the problems he was having like how he was going to have to resolder some components. He'd known the thing wasn't actually ready, but this was more than he'd thought. I let it wash over me as I ate my nutrient powder. My stomach groaned for real food, but I ignored it. Soon, I hoped. Really soon.

The night got darker. We tidied the living room and went one at a time to change. Our routine. I'd kind of hoped the routine might be different with what had happened the previous night and all, but I was okay with this. I was more tired than I was expecting from hiking in the forest, and sleep would be good.

Luke's hands on me would have been better, but you take what you can get in this life.

After Luke was finished, I washed and changed. Normally, when I got back to the bedroom Luke was reading or already drifting into sleep. This time, though, he sat on the edge of his bed. He looked up at me from under sweeping eyelashes.

"Hi," he said, giving me a crooked smile.

"Hi." I took a tentative step forward and perched on the edge of my bed. He leaned right over and put his big, sure hand on my thigh.

Oh. Good.

"I'm not feeling that tired," he said, trailing his fingers up the inseam of my trousers.

"Me neither," I said, throat dry.

He smiled and all I could do was crash forward into him, wrap my arms around him, and crush my lips to his. He took it joyously, laughing and falling back into the bunk with me on top.

It turned out that, while I'd been in the forest, he'd retrieved some lube. The second night I still came first, but I finally got to find out what the weight of his cock felt like in my mouth.

Chapter Thirteen

OVER THE NEXT few days, I made more trips into the forest. Now that I had an idea of the way, it was easy to find the river again, and I found the most efficient route just a little up from where I'd been walking. I ran a string along to mark it, then made a few trips. The water barrels were running down already so I filled them again, carrying two buckets on each trip.

I started using the water I'd got from the river for drinking and cooking and it didn't take long for Luke to give in and help me haul the pump out there. It wasn't like a day away from the array was a great loss for him. He seemed to spend more time cursing at it and taking it into smaller pieces then he did actually putting it together. I very carefully didn't ask, but on days that had extra swearing, I made sure to be more affectionate than usual. That, at least, wasn't a hardship.

I laid the pipe on my own and plumbed it in. It wasn't tough and it was nice to do something that had an actual concrete benefit. I was running every tox screen we had on the food, and it was all coming back clear, but if the look on Luke's face when I spoke about it was anything to go by, we weren't going to be eating anything native any time soon.

I did spend a day with the seed bank, cataloguing and staring wistfully. We had a few hardy strains of wheat, corn, and rice. Someone sentimental had included a small pack of wildflower seed. Then there were the vegetables—tomatoes, cucumbers, peppers, and onions. I looked at them all, my mouth watering. It'd be so easy to take out some seeds and plant them. I wouldn't even need many. I could make a little garden at the edge of the clearing and sow just enough for me and Luke to get away from those terrible nutrient packs.

I didn't though. Luke almost certainly wouldn't go for the idea of literally putting down roots and, I had to admit, a part of me agreed with him. This place was unspoilt and all I could think about was invasive species. The odds were that the plants here would be better adapted than ours; ours might not even grow, but at the same time, I didn't want to risk it. I imagined this world in hundreds of years, all this gone and just fields of wheat remaining.

I didn't want that.

Instead, I found myself pushing further and further into the forest.

It wasn't a conscious choice, but somehow the little worn path I'd worn through to the river started to feel limiting. While there were breaks when I was waiting for results, I found myself drawn back again and again to the river.

It was beautiful. Wide and deep in places, rushing in others. I swear, as it cascaded over the smooth rocks, it almost seemed to chime. The water was somehow bluer than I remember the water being back on Earth, though maybe that shouldn't have surprised me. I knew children drew the sea as blue and that had to have come from somewhere, even if the only sea we saw seemed more of a mucky brown.

Sometimes, I just sat there and watched the water long enough to notice the life. There were tiny brightly coloured fish flitting around when they weren't startled. That was interesting. If they hid when startled, did it imply predators? Where were they?

I kind of wanted to eat the fish, but I knew if fruit was a no, there was no way Luke would agree to fish. They were too small anyway. Not even a mouthful.

I spent days exploring along the bank. It made it easy, gave me a path to follow. I took the cartography tools with me so Luke thought I was using my time sensibly, and I made a map, though it was more to assuage my curiosity than anything else. I went downstream first, and the river got faster and smaller, a few small streams branching out. By the time I'd explored everything I could reach in a reasonable time downstream, Luke had completed the array once and started to pull it to pieces again because it wasn't working.

I limited myself to an hour's walk in case Luke needed me. But I stood there, so often, at the edge of my hour, looking out. I wanted to go on. Wanted to see all the things that had to be out there. I'd catalogued hundreds of insects already, drawing them into my notebook. I'd seen other creatures in the water, something that looked almost like a crayfish once. And the fruit.

Every day I carried back new fruits to test. Every test I did on them came back negative. As far as I could tell, they were safe.

Of course, Luke wanted to wait.

Upriver was initially less exciting, which is to say that it was still deeply thrilling, but the river carried on for a way at much the same depth and speed, and not containing any new fish. The trees around it were the same. I found new insects, of course, but nothing bigger.

I wanted something bigger. I wanted something that was going to blow my mind.

I wanted something good enough that it'd force Luke to stop thinking about the communications array for five minutes and come sit with me in the sun.

I knew it was a long shot. I knew he was doing important work in his own mind, but every day I looked towards the horizon, and I'd think about what I'd seen from the top of the ship and how alone we were. How impossible it'd be for anything to actually reach us even if we got the array working and someone out there actually answered.

I act as though his way of coping was unhealthy, and maybe it was, but maybe my disappearing into the forest wasn't really any healthier. I knew there were things I could do to help him, but I felt sick in the shadow of the ship. I ran as often and as far as I could, slipping into the trees at every opportunity. I only came out to eat and spend time with Luke.

I sometimes wonder, if I'd been the only one who survived, would I have disappeared into the trees entirely.

And so that's how life was, for a while. I ran and hid; Luke worked and swore. We fucked and then lay across from each other in our tiny room, listening to each other breathe and trying to fall asleep.

Chapter Fourteen

IT WAS AN overcast day when I found the clearing.

We'd been having more overcast days. A few had developed into rainstorms, but most of them had cleared up, gone to dump their burden somewhere else.

I woke up to an empty room, as usual. I spent a little time puttering around the place, picking things up and putting them away. The shelter was starting to look more and more lived in. I half-wondered again about expanding it, but mentioning anything to do with rescue and the possibility of it around Luke wasn't generally considered a good idea, so I left it. We'd cope.

I ate, drank a few cups of water, tidied around the bathroom, and took a short shower, then headed out.

Luke stood by the array, frowning. I watched him from a distance. On mornings where things were going well, he'd be happy to see me and greet me with hugs and kisses, which was gratifying. On days when it wasn't going well, he'd tell me he had no time and he had to focus or he'd snap at me.

Of course, most days didn't fall on either extreme.

Luke was frowning, though, that didn't have to mean anything. He was holding a component in his hand, turning it over and over. It didn't look like one of the more operated on and dented pieces of equipment, which meant it was probably one he hadn't taken apart and put back together a million times in his quest to get the array working. A new idea, maybe. That could be good. He'd be feeling optimistic.

He looked up, our eyes met, and he smiled. It seemed like it was safe to talk to him today. I jogged over.

"Hey," I said, carefully dodging the pieces laid out on the tarp. "It's cooler today, Want me to fetch you a jacket?"

"I brought one," he said, nodding over to his work desk. "Not as useless as all that."

"I've never thought you were even a bit useless."

"No, I know," he said, smiling, but his smile was a little tight around the corners. "I mean, hopefully it won't rain anyway."

"I don't know," I said, leaning into his space a little. "I like the rain." Rain meant no exploration, no useful outside work. Luke could carry on working under the shelter, but he normally didn't. Typically, we squashed ourselves onto one tiny bed, limbs tangling together, and listened to the patter of the rain on the roof.

"Insatiable," Luke said, as though it was a problem. His smile seemed more relaxed and genuine, though, so I just smiled and leaned in for a kiss. He returned it happily, running his free hand down my side then around to gently cup my ass. Two could play at that game!

If I started grabbing him, I'd get myself all worked up, then he'd want to get a few hours of work in before the rain started.

"Don't start what you can't finish," I grumbled, then bit gently at his lip. He pulled my closer and I went happily, pushing into him.

If it wasn't for the ship towering over us, I'd say I'd never been happier.

"Okay," he said finally, pulling back a little. "Okay. I'll stop. What are you doing today?"

"What I always do," I said, eyes straying towards my entry point into the forest. The last few days I'd been venturing away from the river. I'd gone as far as I was currently willing to in either direction so instead I'd been going not quite as far then striking out into the forest where I'd map anything that'd be useful to us and draw bugs.

"You're going out?" He frowned and I sighed, reaching up to run a finger down his nose, which made him blink.

"Yes. I'm doing what I always do."

"It might rain."

"Then I'll get wet. I'm sure there's someone around here who'll help me out of my soaking clothes and warm me up."

"You shouldn't joke." Luke frowned. "We don't know just how bad the weather gets. We should be cautious."

"I'm always cautious."

"Alex," he said, and there was a note of pleading in his voice that just went right to my gut. "I don't want you hurt, that's all. Please."

Please. Of course, when he said that, I wasn't going to argue.

"How about this?" I said, leaning in. "I'll go into the forest, but I'll only go a little way. Only a quarter of an hour's walk, max. If it rains, I'll turn around and come right back."

Luke sighed, but I think he understood this was our compromise, because he nodded, then leaned in to kiss my cheek, soft and tender.

"Okay. Straight back if it rains though?"

"I pinkie promise," I said, holding up my pinkie. He laughed but hooked his finger with mine and squeezed, then leaned in for one last sensual kiss before letting go of me and turning back to his work, leaving me to stumble towards the trees.

I didn't go straight in. I went to the hut for my rope and the bag containing my books. I decided to take a quick detour into the lab, but held my breath as I entered the ship like it was a superstition and I believe the ship could steal my soul. I was running some tests on a frozen rat tissue sample we'd brought with us and so far the fruit didn't seem to be harming it.

I was so hungry for something other than nutrient paste. Not in the physical sense, my body was perfectly provided for, but in the spiritual sense. I was dying for other tastes, textures.

When I got into the forest, I did what I told Luke I'd do. I'd pinkie promised, after all, and even if I'd been planning to go back to the particularly big tree I'd found the day before—the one I'd laid a marker on. It could wait. Promises were important, I wasn't going to break mine just because I felt like wandering.

I set out upstream, walked for about ten minutes, then crossed the river. It was particularly wide and shallow there, though the entire stretch I'd found never got big enough that I'd had to do more than roll up my trouser legs. Upstream it was probably deeper.

I stopped to mark a tree and attach my rope to it, then set off walking.

I hadn't walked through many places like this forest in my life. They did still exist on Earth, but they were few and far between and in bad shape. I'd read books, though. Academic books in preparation for the mission, handbooks on how to survive in extreme conditions, and fiction books about adventure. First person accounts of walking through the forest had been the mainstay of my childhood, both those real and those imagined. I could never get enough of them, but they were nothing compared to doing it myself.

Once you got far enough away from the devastation of the landing site, the forest was alive. I didn't see everything, I couldn't, things hid themselves away, but I heard everything. As I walked I was surrounded by an alien song as the native wildlife chirped and called. There was a beetle that made a noise unnervingly like a fork scraping on metal. I'd tracked it down and it looked so benign—small and green and segmented in three—but then it made this sound and I jumped every time I heard it.

Walking into the forest that day, it felt alive with noise. I stood for a while, just far enough away to not hear the stream, and tilted my head back and listened.

It was good to be there, surrounded by the new. I'd never imagined I'd get the chance. If the mission had gone to plan, I'd have been back at base analysing the things brought back by others and figuring out how to exploit the resources of this new planet to keep ourselves alive.

Still, it was lonely. I wished, acutely, that Luke would go with me. That he'd hold my hand as I scrambled up and down banks and over stones. I wouldn't even mind if he laughed at my attempts to climb the trees. I just wanted him to share in my joy at the things that were living all around us.

Maybe, when the array was done, he'd come with me.

I walked, stopping to listen, to breathe, and to marvel at everything. I found another lizard-like thing, different from any I'd seen before, and sat for a while to draw it before carrying on. I let the line I had tied to the path play out behind me, kept smiling and walking.

When I finally stopped, I heard something else just under the sounds of the insects. It sounded like running water.

I glanced back, though there was no way I'd got turned around so the noise couldn't be the river I'd left behind me. That meant....

I moved forward quickly, purposefully. The sound got louder and louder.

Then the trees stopped, and I was in a clearing. A clearing with a drop off in front of me, like the edge of a cliff. A river ran from between the trees. bubbling forward over the exposed ground which gently sloped down on either side to make a valley for it and channelling it to the cliff edge where it disappeared.

A waterfall. I'd come out at the top of a waterfall.

I clasped my hands over my mouth to contain a gasp of delight. I hadn't thought anything like this could be so close to the other river. Our little waterway must be a branch of this one, which was much bigger and faster. I'd seen little waterfalls before, but nothing like this. Not in person.

I stepped forward, and the rope around my waist tugged me back. I'd reached the end.

I looked at it, betrayed. I'd come so much further than I meant to, than I'd promised. Luke would never know, he didn't come into the forest, but I'd promised.

I looked up. The sky was darker and heavier than it had been when I set out. Thunderous. I frowned up at it and bit my lip.

I should go back. Mark my way, come back another time.

But I was so close.

I unfastened the rope from around me and fastened it to the tree instead. I'd find it and find the way back easily enough. I just wanted to look.

I walked up to the edge of the drop.

It wasn't as high as it had seemed from further back, maybe just a little over ten feet. Far enough to hurt myself if I wasn't careful, but I was going to be careful.

The waterfall cascaded down into a small lake, the cliff I was standing on formed the slope that cupped the lake. I followed it around carefully, testing each step. The forest came closer to the edge, then drew back again, leaving a clearing at the bottom of the slope, leading right down to the water. The lake wasn't large, but the water was clear and it looked so good, I wanted to wade into it, to swim. I bet it'd be cool—not that I needed cool on such an overcast day.

It was beautiful though. The rock cliff had a subtle, purple sheen to it. The lake was clear, and I could see creatures darting around in it, some much larger than anything I'd seen so far. The waterfall was gorgeous, tumbling clear like there was a natural cave behind it.

I wanted to explore. I itched to explore. I might have, but as I took a step forward, a raindrop fell.

I looked down at my arm where it had landed, feeling betrayed by the weather that was turning on me just when I'd made this new discovery. Then another one landed. Then another.

Shit.

I'd promised I'd go back if it rained. Luke had been worried and I'd promised him. I'd said I wouldn't come too far and I'd turn back as soon as it rained. He was going to be waiting for me and I'd got too caught up and gone too far.

The heavens opened.

My trip back up the slope was quicker than my one down it, though, I was still careful to watch where I put my feet. Luke would be even more upset if I hurt myself.

Finding the tree wasn't hard and I untied the rope and wrapped it around myself. Of course, by then, I was soaked to the bone but that was okay. That was fine. When I got back, I'd get dry, and Luke would hold me and make me feel better. Unless he was pissed at me and decided to sleep in the ship or something.

I had to get back.

This time, walking back through the forest, I didn't stop to listen or to watch. I kept my eyes front and centre as much as I could, trying to focus only on where I was putting my feet. I'd slipped a few times while exploring, but I couldn't afford to now.

I'd been such an idiot, not paying attention to where I was or how far I'd have to go to get back home. I'd been so caught up in my little dream of being an explorer. I'd just been running and not thinking.

The line reeled in as I walked. At least it was easier walking back, I wasn't distracted by every little thing I walked past. It was still raining, the natural sounds of the forest drowned out by the thump of raindrops against the leaves of the trees. They were angled so rain streamed along them, drenching me and the ground— even though I was theoretically under cover.

If anything, the rain was getting worse. It was heavier than we'd seen it before.

It was so heavy, in fact, I almost missed the shouting.

"Alex."

My name. I froze for a second. It couldn't be. I was imagining it.

"Alex."

Shit.

"Luke?" I called back, hurrying forward. He was shouting my name as I pushed past some bushes and spotted him standing on my path, rope in one hand and leaning against a tree. His entire side was splattered with dull mud and he was holding himself awkwardly.

Shit.

"Luke," I said, hurrying towards him. "What the hell are you doing here?"

"You didn't come back," he said, and I couldn't tell if he was angry or in pain, but either way it was my fault. "You said you were only going a little way."

Shit.

"I'm sorry," I said, quickly. I reached out to grab his free hand. "I got distracted. I didn't mean to."

"I know, I know," he said, words short, clipped. "I... I fell."

"You're covered in mud."

"I hurt my ankle. I don't think it's too bad. I just..."

"Oh, god," I said, and he looked at me sharply. "I'm just... I didn't mean this. I'm so sorry. I didn't..."

"Look, I know," he said. He reached out and grabbed me with one mud-smeared hand. I could see how, under the mud, the skin was scuffed. We had to get him clean. There could any number of microorganisms in the mud. Any number of potential diseases.

He was going to die. Die or hate me, and either way, I was going to be there alone in the shadow of all my dead friends.

"Hey," Luke said, and he sounded like he was making an effort so my voice would sound level, less strained. "I need you right now, Alex. I need your help. Help me back to the clearing."

For one hysterical moment I thought he meant the clearing I'd just found, but no. He meant back to the ship. And that made sense. At the ship, I could clean him up, get him warm and, maybe, undo the damage I'd done.

"Okay," I said, stepping into his side. He sighed and seemed to relax a little, throwing his arm around my shoulder and letting me take some of his weight.

He was warm against me which was comforting. I let myself grip handfuls of his T-shirt to ground myself. It was slow going, manoeuvring back to the stream, but we were careful. A few metres out from the stream, we passed a skid mark on the path where he had fallen.

He kicked at the skid mark then winced and I had to bite back a smile.

We stopped at the edge of the stream for him to rest and for me to untie the line, then we carried on back downstream and out along the path I'd trodden into the dirt, the one I'd walked so many times before.

The burnt clearing caused by our ship was treacherous to cross in the rain, but we made it into the shelter and got the door shut. I fumbled around a minute, getting the lights turned on. The rain was so loud it sounded it like would break the roof apart. Luke just stood there in the middle of the room, wet and dejected, holding his foot gingerly off the floor.

I wanted to cry, but if I gave in and started, we'd just be stuck there, wet and cold forever.

"Okay," I said. "Let's get you clean."

He blinked at me, and I realised he wasn't going to be able to hear me above the pounding of the rain, but that was okay. I stepped up into his space—which honestly wasn't hard in the tiny living area—and tugged at his T-shirt. He got the idea and helped to peel it off, balling it up and throwing it into the corner.

I unfastened his trousers and pulled them down, something I'd done many times by this point, but this time his skin was cool and clammy under my fingers. He sat bare-assed on one of the chairs and I grabbed his feet, pulled them into my lap to free him from his boots and trousers until he was sat there naked.

His ankle was swollen and angry looking, but it wasn't at an unnatural angle or anything; while he winced when I took his shoe off, he didn't scream. My best guess without dragging him into the ship to x-ray it was a sprain. That was good. Well, not good, but he wouldn't die, and he wouldn't leave me alone.

Looking at it, I felt tears threatening. It was okay. He was going to be okay.

He reached over and grabbed my hand. I looked up, startled, and he was saying something that I couldn't hear over the pounding of the rain. I shook my head and he just reached for me. I moved forward so he could touch me, gently cradle my face and lean down to kiss me. He stroked my cheek like he was as glad I was alive as I was.

I stripped quickly and efficiently, then helped Luke to his feet. I tried not to let it worry me when he let me take his body weight. It was good that he let me help.

The pounding of the rain on the roof carried on drowning out any sound, so we washed in silence. He let me direct him under the showerhead, run shampoo through his hair, and cover him with soap. I got to feel as his body slowly warm up again and become pliant under my hands as he relaxed. I helped him limp back out of the shower and grabbed a quick one myself while he dried, glad we'd installed the pump as, even with the downfall, I didn't think our primitive shower system would have stood up to much use.

I got out of the shower quickly. Luke was sitting, towel slung around his hips, studying his own ankle. He moved it experimentally, winced, but then shrugged as though it wasn't as bad as he'd expected. I let out a breath.

He was going to be okay.

I grabbed a towel and dried quickly before dodging back into the bedroom for some T-shirts and underwear to sleep in. I spun around to go back to the bathroom and jumped to see Luke had followed me.

This close he looked tired and strained. Maybe his foot would be okay, but that didn't mean he wasn't going to be mad at me. I'd broken my promise, after all. Following me was what made him hurt himself. He'd be right to be cross.

Still, I didn't know how I'd bear it if he was. I didn't know how I'd cope if he left me here in this place.

I hoped some of what I was feeling showed on my face since it was too loud to say it. Maybe it did because his expression seemed to soften. He reached up to cup my cheek, then leaned in and brushed a soft kiss across my forehead. Something inside me curled in joy at the tenderness of it, and I couldn't fight down a smile.

Slowly, we made our way into the bedroom. He sat heavily on the bed and looked at his foot again. It was swelling more. It'd need some support.

The full first aid kit was back over in the ship, but I had enough with me in the house. I fetched bandages and he seemed relieved to see them. I sat on my bunk and he easily stretched his leg across the gap and lay it in my lap. I squeezed his calf reassuringly and set to work wrapping it. I was biotech staff, not medical, but every person on the ship was well drilled in first aid.

When I was done, Luke, still naked, took his leg back and manoeuvred to lie down. I didn't blame him, since somehow it seemed to be hotter now than it was before the heavens opened. He looked good, laid out like that. My dick twitched.

I shifted, wishing I'd got dressed at least. Luke's eyes were closed but I didn't want him to open them and see my inappropriate boner.

I still wasn't convinced he wasn't going to be pissed at me later, though, he didn't seem to be right now.

He slid his eyes open and I angled myself away from him slightly. I needed space. I stood and went back to the main room, quickly thinking of every disgusting thing I could as I fetched a glass of water and some pain pills. I thought about what might have happened to us both out there. I thought about the spaceship towering over us, full of my dead loved ones.

I thought about Luke among them. My mind kept coming back to the idea that he could have taken a worse fall and been really injured or, even worse, died. What would I even do with him? Drag him back into the ship and freeze him? There'd be no chance of digging graves for them all on my own unless that'd be my last act and I'd be able to just lie down next to them and die too. Or maybe I'd stay here, going slowly insane in my hut in the shadow of everyone I ever loved. Maybe I'd head out into the forest, eat some poison berry, and die alone under a log. Nobody would ever find me.

I realised my limbs were shaking. I was probably in shock, or something like it. I forced myself to sit down, to lean my elbows against my thighs and breathe. I followed the rise and fall of my breath, counting to ten over and over again. I had to get it together. Luke was the one who was hurt, the one who'd been let down. I couldn't fall to pieces on him.

By the time I went back to him, I wasn't hard anymore.

He smiled at me, took the pills and the water, and drank, setting the glass back on the side before reaching for me. I was more than happy to crawl up on the bunk next to him and settle into his arms. There wasn't really space, but I pressed in close against him and lay my head on his shoulder. He stroked my back gently and it felt wonderful.

He was safe. The ankle would be an annoyance, but he was here and safe. I'd broken my promise, but it didn't seem to have hurt us. If we'd both been hurt out there, it could have been a disaster. We were so vulnerable. There were a million ways I could lose him and be trapped here alone. I didn't want that. I'd do anything to avoid that.

He said something, I could feel his jaw moving against my head, but the rain was still too loud to hear. I tightened my arms around him.

I hadn't meant to sleep—not really—but with Luke warm and close and the rain beating out a rhythm on the roof, I never stood a chance.

Chapter Fifteen

I WOKE TO the quiet, my back aching. The bunk really wasn't big enough for the two of us, and I had kind of twisted around Luke to make it work. It was still a good feeling to not wake up alone. His skin against my cheek, the closeness and realness of him, almost made the pain worth it. I almost considered ignoring my body and just settling down to sleep again. My limbs were so heavy. It was quiet, finally. I had a day of apologising and working to fix anything the rain had ruined ahead of me, and I wanted this closeness, this peace.

Then my back twinged and, with a sigh, I rolled out of the bunk. I was as careful as I could be, but when I glanced back, Luke's eyes were drifting open. Shit.

"Hey," I said, reaching down to stroke his hair. "Everything's fine, go back to sleep."

He blinked at me, then raised his hand to touch my cheek. He smiled. "I'm glad you're okay."

This boy. This stupid boy. I'd scared him. He was worried about me, and he'd been trying to check on me when he hurt himself.

"I'm okay," I promised, taking his hand and kissing his fingers. He smiled a dopey smile and it made me ache. It made me wish we weren't the only people in the world so I could know his smile was really for me. I trusted him enough to know he genuinely cared, I wasn't just a convenience to him, but that didn't do much to quieten the voice in the back of my head. I couldn't avoid the nagging feeling that, if we'd all landed and there were hundreds of beautiful men and women walking around here, he'd never have looked at me twice.

"Sleep."

"Stay," Luke said, tugging at me gently.

"I can't." I kissed his fingers again. "The bed's too narrow. I'll just be here."

He frowned like he'd never considered the beds being too small to hold two before. Then he let go of me, and I turned and climbed into my own bed. I settled in and turned to see him watching me with half-lidded eyes.

It was easy to reach out and find his hand again, still hanging in the gap between us. He squeezed my finger.

"Alex," he said, voice slurred with sleep. "I'm glad you're here. I don't want to be alone."

"Me too," I said softly, into the night. His eyes were already closed and he didn't say anything else, just lay there and let his breathing slowly even out as he slid into sleep.

This time, it took me a long time to follow him.

Chapter Sixteen

"SO, I THINK it's just sprained."

"I think so too," I said, finishing off the bandage around his ankle. It looked better than it had the previous night, though, the natural light might have helped with that.

Just sprained was good. Just sprained meant, in a couple of days, he'd be up and walking around like nothing had happened, and I could stop feeling a squeezing in my gut every time I looked at him.

Maybe some of that feeling was showing through on my face because Luke leaned forward and cupped my cheeks. It made it so I had to look up at him, something I'd been trying to avoid. So far that day, I'd been over to the ship twice for supplies and out to the shelter to check all the pieces for Luke's array, traipsing backwards and forwards over the rain-soaked ground just to avoid having to look into Luke's face and know he was angry with me.

"Hey," he said, stroking my cheek. "What's wrong?"

"Nothing. Do you want me to bring you some of the pieces of the array in here to work on? I don't know if there'll be enough light."

"Alex..."

"I mean, I can help you move over there but the floor's kind of slippery with mud, and I don't want you to hurt yourself because of me again so..."

"Alex," Luke said, louder this time, more firmly. "Will you please just stop for a second and talk to me?"

I stopped and looked up at him. I hadn't thought this through, kneeling in front of him. It made me feel small, caught. I couldn't get up and run without jostling his foot where it lay in my lap and, but looking up into his eyes; I wasn't sure I wanted to. In fact, I wasn't sure I didn't want him to just pin me there and pull all my secrets out of me.

"Okay."

"Good," Luke said, smiling softly. He leaned forward and stroked the side of my face gently. "You think this is your fault?"

"I think," I said, carefully, "that if I'd only gone as far as I promised, and came back when I promised, you wouldn't have gone looking for me."

"Yeah," Luke said, and he frowned a little. Shit, maybe he hadn't been mad at me, but he was going to be now I'd pointed out what an idiot I'd been. "I mean, yeah, my being in there was your fault. That doesn't make my falling your fault. I was... I was worried. I wasn't really looking where I was going and I tripped. I should have been more careful; I'm not exactly experienced with wild places."

"You were worried?"

I was probably pushing my luck, but I needed to hear it now, in the light of day. He smiled at me, eyes crinkling, and brushed his fingers along my jaw. "Yes, I was worried about you. You didn't come back, I thought you might have fallen."

"I should have come back..."

"Maybe," he said with a shrug. "I mean, I'm not an idiot, I half expected you to go further than you promised."

I shifted a little, heat spreading up my neck and across my cheeks. Of course, he'd noticed me running away into the forest at every opportunity, but I hadn't really acknowledged that to myself. I definitely hadn't let myself contemplate what he must think about my running away every five seconds.

"I didn't mean to, I got distracted."

"Find a new beetle?"

"A waterfall," I said, blushing a little more, but Luke was still smiling and stroking my cheek. "I could hear it and I followed the noise. It's only a little thing, but it was in this little clearing. It was beautiful."

A good place to build a house. The thought seemed to spring up in my mind fully formed. My little lake with a house we built together. One with actual windows and a big bed we could share together without hurting our backs. I thought of myself, standing there in the doorway in the light of the morning sun, looking out over the lake with Luke's big, strong hands on my hips, pulling me back against his chest.

It was a nice dream. Impossible, of course. I thought Luke would probably carry on looking for other people until we died. Even if we'd landed like we were meant to, if we were building a real civilisation here, it would have been impossible. Luke would have been too busy to even look twice at me. I'd have been stuck on the ship doing tests on local samples, checking for toxicity. Maybe I'd have shared a room with Eileen, let her cover for me again until we were more fully settled.

It occurred, then, I hadn't even thought of her since the night before when the rain had started.

I was the worst.

"Hey," Luke said, his voice tugging at my attention. "Where've you gone? Tell me about your waterfall."

"There's no time for that," I said, standing quickly. "We have work to do."

I didn't give him a chance to protest, slipping into the dark of the bedroom to grab us both jackets. When I came back out, he didn't say anything, just took the jacket and slipped it on.

I'd ruined the mood, of course. I knew I would.

Better to get us focused on work before Luke realised he wouldn't have been rushing through the forest and he wouldn't have slipped, if he hadn't been worrying about me in the first place.

"I think it'll be easier if you help me outside," Luke said. I nodded and moved to him. He wasn't that much bigger than me so helping him to his feet wasn't so bad. I had to put my arm around him to help him across the slightly uneven muddy ground to the communications array.

As I settled him in a chair, I stopped to actually look at the thing for the first time in a while. It looked like it'd been put together and taken apart again a few times. Pieces were bent, missing, and scuffed.

As a physical representation of Luke's hope, the array was looking a little battered. I could only cross my fingers that the hope inside him was in better shape.

"So," Luke said, drawing my attention back to him. "Look, I know you can't really deal with this right now, but I'm going to need your help."

"I can deal with it," I said, which was a blatant enough lie that he did me the favour of not commenting on it.

"I think I've nearly got everything working. Or at least I'm at the stage of putting it all back together. There are some things I can do from here, but a lot of it I'm going to need to stand up."

"You know I don't actually know what I'm doing, right? I'm a scientist, not an engineer."

"I just need you to follow directions."

I nodded. I could take direction.

He smiled at me gently, like I'd agreed to something bigger. Perhaps I had. I wasn't going to be able to run away into the forest for a few days. I was going to stay here and help Luke move around, help him finish this array. Maybe it'd work this time; someone would answer and they'd have a way to get to us or a way for us to get to them.

Perhaps Luke's hope wouldn't have been for nothing. I hoped it hadn't.

"Okay," I said, putting my hands on my hips. "You can't yell at me if I ask questions though. Deal?"

"Deal."

"Great. So, where do we start?"

Chapter Seventeen

IT TURNED OUT we started with me sitting, watching as he unsoldered and resoldered a circuit board. Predictably, it wasn't very exciting.

"So," I said, leaning forward to rest my chin on my arms. We were sitting on opposite sides of the table he had set up under the gazebo for him to work on. Not for the first time, I wished the thing had sides so I didn't have to see the ship. I'd brought this on myself though. I'd cope. "You told me it wasn't quite finished yet but..."

"I think they rushed the construction," Luke grumbled. "I can't get it to work anyway. I mean, I got it to turn on last time so at least we're getting close, but it wasn't transmitting, and that's kind of the point of it."

"And you know how to fix that kind of problem?"

"I know how to fix everything." I looked up at him, ready to be sarcastic, but he was grinning like he'd made a great joke and I found myself smiling back. He really did have a disarming smile. He'd smiled at me a few times back on Earth, before we'd left. It had even been a problem back then.

"Is that what they teach you in command school?"

"Oh, definitely," he said. "Hours and hours on radio repair."

"Well, it's a good job you survived to help me," I said, carefully nudging his good foot under the table. "Just think how much trouble I'd be in if I'd been stuck here with a chemist or something."

"Terrible," Luke deadpanned. "The worst."

"So, you're just picking your way through this and hoping for the best?"

"I mean, yeah." He shrugged. "I have the manual but, honestly, the manual stopped being helpful a long time ago. I do know a little about circuitry though. I know you were joking, but that is the kind of thing they taught us at command school. I was meant to be part of the team running this mission, making all the high-level decisions. I was meant to have all the skills to make whatever call needed to be made, which meant knowing everything from how to solder a circuit board right up to command overrides for the onboard weapons system."

"We have weapons?"

"We'd hoped the planet was unoccupied but you know how quickly we had to move once we found the place. Normal caution went out of the window."

I nodded, because I did know. It didn't seem like ten minutes between the finding of an earth-like planet surprisingly near to actual Earth and the call for people to be trained. Still, I didn't like to think we'd meant to wipe out whatever life was here. The fact life was there at all seemed amazing. I couldn't imagine doing anything to endanger it.

"So, how much did you actually know about this planet before we left?"

Command had always been vague about that. They'd said it was habitable but they'd never really committed beyond that. They'd said there were variable ecosystems and given us training in everything Earth had to offer and we'd just accepted it. It had seemed better than the alternative.

"Perhaps it's best we don't talk about this."

"Who do you think I'm going to tell?"

"Well, you might tell whoever comes to rescue us?"

"I won't," I said. Nobody was coming, so it was an easy promise. Impulsively, I leaned over the table and offered him my pinkie. He looked at it for a second like I was crazy and I hoped he wasn't thinking of my last pinkie promise, the one I broke when I went too far into the forest, but then he offered me his own finger. I grinned and linked our pinkies together. "Pinkie promise."

"Are these legally binding?" he asked, but he seemed to relax a fraction at my silliness. "Okay, if you want the truth, we didn't really know anything."

"Nothing?"

"We suspected there was liquid water which would imply a temperature humans could survive at. We were at least fifty percent certain there was an atmosphere and it was going to be breathable."

"Fifty percent."

"It was an estimate."

I'd known, of course, there was a chance we'd land, and there'd be nothing. Everyone had known. I remembered my mum's initial horror that we were even going to try this. That we were going to go out into space and try this, that we'd put ourselves forward. The recruiters had been very positive, sold it up, but she kept asking me again and again how they knew it would be safe, how they knew it was habitable, and I hadn't been able to answer her. I'd seen reports later, full of physics I didn't understand, and I'd trusted the science. There'd been the flu breakout and the rising sea level and mum had stopped asking, then. I don't think she ever trusted in the mission in the way I did, but she realised staying on Earth wasn't going to work out.

Maybe I should have listened to her more. I'd still be dead, but maybe I should have stayed there and died with her. Maybe we should have all stayed there.

No point dwelling on it, we were here.

"You must have really wanted off the planet, to face that head-on and go anyway," I said, trying to turn focus back on Luke. It was easier to think about why he might be here than when I'd lost.

"I didn't believe Earth was going to last much longer. I did what I had to."

I nodded and risked a glance back up at the ship. It was looming there, dark and ominous. I wondered, not for the first time, if a few more checks wouldn't have saved them. I'd been in officer training since I was fourteen, known most of these people for that long. If we'd just been slower, more cautious.

But then maybe if we'd been slower, none of us would have made it off the Earth. Not that two men alone had much chance of saving a species. We were it, now. I suppose the best we could hope was that someday there would be intelligent life on this planet, that I'd evolve and find some remnant of us buried in the rock and they'd know, at least, that once upon a time, other beings existed in the universe.

"God, this is depressing," I said, shaking my head. "I didn't mean to start all this. Tell me something else. Anything else."

"I don't know," he said. There was a tightness around his eyes and I hated that I'd put it there. "What do you want me to tell you?"

"I don't know. I guess... your first kiss! Tell me about your first kiss."

"Really?" he said, and a blush was starting to colour his cheeks. This had to be a good story.

"Yes. Come on, Mister I-Know-Everything. Did you have time at command school for making out or was I your first?"

"I'm thirty-two. You're not my first."

"So, tell me."

For a second, I thought he was going to refuse; then his eyes seemed to drift to the ship. Maybe he was thinking the kind of thoughts I was because when his eyes came back to mine, he nodded.

"Fine. But when we're found, you can't tell anyone else."

"You already made me pinkie promise."

"That was about confidential government information. This is much worse."

"Well, you have to tell me now."

"So, her name was Valerie. She was on the command track, of course."

"Oh, of course!"

"Do you want to hear the story or not?"

I mimed zipping my lips closed and he smiled a secret, warm kind of smile. The kind of smile that wasn't mean for PR or to calm and charm the people under his command, but the one that seemed to be saved just for me. I mean, all his smiles were just for me then since we were, as far as we knew, the only ones alive in the world, but this one was different. It felt different.

"Okay, so, command school was serious business, you know? I left my family to go to command school at eight. My parents died young, but my gran was a pretty high-level civil servant and my grandad was a lawyer so they had the money and the power to get me straight onto the command track.

"Growing up in command track was pretty weird. We used to get two weeks at Christmas to go home and two weeks in the summer, but other than that, we were at school. And every year, more people were moved down to regular track. People who couldn't handle it. It... well, I think you can guess it didn't create a great environment. We were constantly in competition. We knew only so many people would end up actually commanding ships.

"Valerie was always really bad at that, being cut-throat. I mean, I was, too, when it came down to it. We were both co-operators and that worked out for me in the long run. They eventually weeded out all the people who'd use the chance to be in a position of power on a new planet to hurt others and establish some kind of cult of personality, but when we were in our early teens, it just hurt. I mean, I'm told that age is pretty brutal, anyway, but in command school...

"Anyway, it turns out the reason they let it go on at all was they wanted to test for 'mental fortitude,' whatever the hell that is. And Valerie didn't have it. I was thirteen and she was fourteen when she got sent down. She cried a lot, those last few weeks, and I spent a lot of time sitting with her, holding her hand, encouraging her to carry on. I guess that's some of the behaviour that ended up with them marking me down for the command track.

"Valerie, though, she got called into the office and told she was being sent down to train as a normal crew member. She left on the American ship, I think. When she came back to get her things, she took me aside and held my hand and, well, I was a thirteen-year-old boy. I was ninety-eight percent hormones. She held my hands, looked me right in the eye, and told me I was the kindest man she knew, then she kissed me."

"Oh, gosh," I said, leaning my head in my hands. "That's all kind of romantic."

"I mean, for me, it kind of came out of nowhere. I'd thought we were just friends. I didn't realise until later that it meant goodbye."

"It's sweet. Did you stay in touch?"

"No," he said, quirking his lip. "She never asked. I think she wanted the clean break. I thought about her sometimes, but, well, you know how it is."

"I do," I sighed. With the best of intentions and the most intense of teenage loves he probably still wouldn't have had time. We'd had more relaxation time than it sounded like he did, longer periods of home-leave definitely, but we were still too busy for maintaining long distance relationships.

In a way, it explained how he was able to be so calm about losing people. He was used to the people in his life not staying around and to having to cope without them, to them dropping out of his life and never coming back, of having no control over that process. In a way, it only made it admirable that he could be so warm, so open. He really was extraordinary.

"I would maybe have tried, but I don't think I slept for most of my teenage years. For all the strings my grandparents pulled to get me onto the command track, I had to be damn good to stay there. It felt like I had a private tutor before I could walk. But you must know that because you got into the programme too."

"Well, yes," I said, my eyes darting to the ship. "We could never afford anything like that—not after my dad died—but I had a friend who really wanted to get into the programme, and her parents didn't mind me sitting in on her tutoring sessions."

He glanced over to the ship too, opened his mouth, closed it again. There was nothing he could say to that, I knew, but absurdly I wished there were. Wished there was some nugget of insight they'd given him in command school that would let him turn around to me now and know just what to say to make this better.

"Anyway," he said, gently kicking me under the table. "That was my first kiss. I'm not sure it counts, though, since she kind of just bestowed it on me and walked away."

"All kisses count," I said, trying to sound playful again. It was probably a little flat. "If that one doesn't, what's your first kiss that does count, then?"

"Well, that one's probably worse. See, the thing was, in command school being brilliant was the norm. I don't mean to brag, you know, but before command school most of my social credit came from being someone who might be good enough to get into command school. After I got there..."

"You're not seriously trying to convince me you were some kind of social outcast, are you?"

"Puberty was kind to me," he said, and I couldn't imagine him not being beautiful at any age. If I'd met him as a teenager, even if we were both covered in acne and only half-grown into our limbs, I was sure I'd still throw myself at his feet.

"We spent most of our time working, but we had these scheduled socialisation things."

"Oh, god, we had them too. Like your primary school disco only with more hormones."

"Yeah. I mean, I don't know who they put in charge of those things, but we used to have crepe paper streamers and fruit punch."

"We had themed ones. I remember a beach disco where we all went in our swimming gear. God, that was the height of teenage embarrassment, trying to dance with a super hot boy you really liked while wearing regulation swimming trunks."

Luke laughed. "We never did that at least. It was all super highbrow. The boys were expected to wear pants, not jeans, you know. And they did formal dances. Oh, god, it was terrible.

"There was this other boy on the command track, Arjun, and he was gorgeous. He was one of those people who puberty kind of blew lightly over him and seemed to transform him overnight from a child to a beautiful man without any pain. I was there with limbs too long for my body and ears that stuck out. and he looked like he should be on a catwalk."

"I can't imagine you with ears sticking out," I said, reaching across the table to flick them. "I bet it was really cute, though. Did he sweep you off your feet?"

"No, not in any way. I was trying to be cool, but one of my friends knew I liked him. And one of his friends knew my friend, so there was this weird telephone line of friends passing messages up and down the dance hall. He couldn't just come down and talk to me, and I'd never be able to just walk up and talk to him.

"So, this train of friends finally worked out he didn't mind looking at me and he'd meet me in the boy's toilets in fifteen minutes.

"They were, I kid you not, the worst fifteen minutes of my life. I kept looking at him, hoping he'd look at me, but he never did, and I started thinking maybe one of the friends got confused somewhere in the chain and he actually hated me, or he wanted to make out with someone else. But I went along anyway at the right time and went into the bathroom.

"It felt like I was waiting in there for ages. I'd almost given up, then he walked in like some kind of prince. He looked me up and down and said something like 'so, do you want to kiss with tongue or without?' and I was like 'with?' and then he stepped right up and kissed me, like he did it all the time. And he probably did. Mostly what I remember was that it was wet. With the benefit of hindsight, it probably wasn't the greatest kiss in the world. At the time it felt like Disney stuff. Like birds singing and happily ever after."

"I know that feeling," I said. "Were you boyfriends then?"

He snorted. "No. He stepped back, said 'okay,' then turned and walked out of the room. I don't think I ever exchanged another word with him. A half hour later, he was in there again with another boy."

"That piece of shit," I gasped.

"My teenage heart was broken. I mooned about him for days."

"Entire days?"

"Well, things always moved quickly in command school. We didn't have much time for moping."

"You wouldn't, everything you have to learn. If you had dated him, you'd probably have misplaced him under a pile of papers and he'd have been lost forever."

"Probably," Luke laughed, rubbing his ankle against mine. "What about you? Come on, you've got two first kiss stories out of me now, I want one of yours."

"Well, I only have one," I said. "And it's not as good a story. It was just Ramsey. He was a friend. We were, like, the two shy, quiet ones who hung out at the edge of the social group, so when there were room parties or organised fun or whatever we'd ended up on the edge of them together.

"We were just hanging out one day, chatting, and he told me about this crush he had that he was shy to ask out. They were really popular and he didn't want to get turned down by them. So, I talked him up, told him how smart and kind he was. He said he couldn't ask because he'd never been kissed, and it was embarrassing."

"Alex, were you his teacher?"

"Oh, quiet," I said, flushing. "It wasn't like that. He just needed a friend and I'm good at being a friend. I held his hand and told him it was okay because I hadn't been kissed either. Then, he looked at me with those big, gorgeous dark eyes of his and said maybe we could help each other."

"How sweet."

"It really was," I said, shaking my head a little. "Neither of us really knew what we were doing. We were soft and careful with each other, barely touching. I'm surprised I didn't burn up from blushing."

"And were you his boyfriend after that?" Luke asked, his tone light and teasing as he echoed my words from earlier.

"Oh, shush. No. He still liked the other person, and I liked him but not like that. We were friends for ages after, until he dropped out of the programme." At the time, it had been devastating. Command had decided he was psychologically unfit, too prone to anxiety and depression. I couldn't help but look at him and think how similar we'd always been, wondering if I wasn't too prone to anxiety or depression.

Now, I was here. If he hadn't dropped out, he'd almost certainly be dead. He was dead, of course. We'd been asleep long enough that everyone we knew was dead even if there was still life on Earth, but I hoped he'd enjoyed the extra time not being on the ship had given him.

"So, I don't have to worry that he was on one of the other ships, and he's going to come over the horizon and sweep you away."

"Hardly," I snorted. "Come on, are you done with that circuit board yet?"

"Yes, actually," Luke said, holding it out to me. "I was done a few minutes ago, but I wanted your story. Come on, let me show you how it attaches, then maybe we can recreate some of those first kisses."

"Oh, no way," I said, letting the distraction work. "We can do a lot better than that."

Chapter Eighteen

WE SPENT THE next three days working like that—chatting, spending time, ignoring the ship looming over us in the background, stopping too often to fuck. Honestly, my skin itched the entire time and I'd have happily run away into the forest and not come back, but Luke needed me.

Actually spending time with Luke was nice too. After the kissing conversation, we mostly stuck to early history—who we'd been before we entered into the programme. After all, there weren't too many stories I could tell about my adulthood or teenage years that didn't involve someone lying dead in the ship behind me. Not that most of my childhood stories didn't involve Eileen, but I found that the more I talked about her, the calmer I felt about it. When I pulled up the old memories, they lay over the screaming pain of her death, muting it a little.

It still hurt like hell, but not as much as it had. Not enough so I felt like I didn't know how to breathe whenever I thought about her.

On the third morning, Luke tried to convince me he was better by walking on his ankle without wincing like it really hadn't been too bad, and I didn't have to worry anymore.

I ignored him and carried on helping. By that point, I'd done enough that I wanted to see it through. When I told him, he smiled.

The fourth day of my working on the array dawned crisp and bright. We ate, cleaned, and then made our way over to the array.

"We can probably finish this today," Luke said, picking up one of the pieces we'd been working on. "If we push. What do you think?"

I thought, whatever happened next, everything was about to change. If this didn't work, if it didn't even turn on, well, I wasn't sure what Luke would do next but I was sure it wouldn't be good. Surely he wouldn't be able to keep on just keeping on, pretending things were going to work out and going through the motions of taking it all apart and putting it back together.

But then, if it did turn on and nobody replied, things would change. He'd have to face it, and I wasn't sure he was ready for that. I wasn't sure I was ready for that. If someone did reply, well, they'd be so far away. What then? Would we try to go to them? If we did, if we travelled for months or years and found other humans, what then? What if I'd been wrong? What if people did notice us and they'd been on the way this entire time, just a little too far away for me to see from the top of the ship? What then? Would he still want me when there were other people? Would we drift apart until this felt like just a bad dream? Would I have to carry on and pretend nothing had happened here, that my entire world hadn't been torn to pieces.

Things were going to change, and I couldn't stop them. There was only one answer I could give to Luke.

"Let's do it."

Chapter Nineteen

RESOLVE WAS VERY grand, but the day was actually quite dull. More soldering. More quiet, hopeful stories told. Bits of our lives shared. I watched him work a lot, tried to focus on that and not on my swirling mess of emotions.

Every so often, I'd be allowed to help with something. To put a piece in place or something simple. It's probably pathetic how happy I was to do those things for him, but he seemed so happy I was there with him. That I was taking an interest. It was hard not to get swept up in his hope. His certainty that we were going to do this. That we were going to make this work.

And then, I had applied the last piece and slid the last panel slid back into place. I stood back and wiped my hands on my trousers then looked over at Luke who was sat at the control panel.

"Done?" he asked, fiddling with the edges of the panel, a nervous gesture that was as reassuring as it was endearing. I nodded, trying to play it cool though my stomach was rebelling. I moved over to stand next to him.

The panel was dark. He took a shuddering breath, then reached out and wrapped his arms around me. I let my eyes fall closed. Let myself absorb the heat of his body pressing close to mine. This was it. This was the moment when everything would change, or wouldn't.

Maybe that was going to be the rest of our lives.

He squeezed me tight, fingers digging into my hips, then pulled back a little. He turned and looked at the panel. He raised a hand, ran it slowly along the edge, then hit the power button.

The panel lit up. We'd gotten this much right, at least. It wasn't a high-tech thing, dials and leads and a liquid crystalline output display. A microphone hung off the edge of it and a speaker was strapped precariously to its side. It was almost insulting, how basic it looked.

"Okay," Luke said, "let's see if it works."

He threw a switch, carefully adjusted one of the dials. Then he stepped back from me and grabbed a small handheld radio from the table. He took it, tuned it, whispered something that might have been a prayer, and then turned it on.

The radio picked up the signal. Played it. It was in Morse code, and it was a long time since I'd practised, but I knew the signal anyway: our ship's registration and our current coordinates according to the ship's instruments.

We were broadcasting.

"It's working," Luke said, almost as though he didn't believe it.

"Yes," I agreed, stepping up to it again. "It's working." Anyone out there now would be able to hear us. As long as they turned to emergency frequency, at least. Checking emergency frequency was standard. I imagined a very board American, manning the radio somewhere outside our forest being jolted into life by our signal. Running to her commander. Jumping in cars. Making their way to us.

I turned and hid my face in Luke's shoulder. We'd turned it on. There was no going back now.

If there was anyone on the planet, they were coming for us.

Chapter Twenty

I WOKE UP the next morning to a warm body pressed against mine. I grumbled and turned, trying to hide my face, but Luke just laughed and pulled at my shoulder until I rolled back over—as much as I could roll in my tiny bunk— to look at him.

"What time is it?" I grumbled. He shoved a mug of nutrient paste into my hands and I groaned again. "And who do I have to kill to get some real food?"

"Soon," he said. "I can't pick up any kind of returned signal yet, but they might not even send a signal. They might just arrive. Eat your nutrient paste."

I did as I was told. It still tasted vaguely like hydrated chalk. If I could have, right then, I'd have probably grabbed some local fruit and jammed it into my mouth just to have a different taste. I knew the nutrient paste kept me alive but my body didn't understand why we couldn't have a roast instead with thick gravy and fluffy mashed potatoes.

I wondered if any of the local plants had edible tubers. Probably not, and even if they did Luke wouldn't let me eat them, but it might be worth checking.

At least, if we were rescued, they might have better food.

"Why are you even waking me up?" I asked. Normally, he left me to sleep.

"No reason, it's just a lovely day."

"Almost every day here is lovely," I said suspiciously.

"Exactly! So, we should go out and enjoy it. You should go out and enjoy it. There's a wide world out there. You shouldn't be stuck in the camp. You should be exploring."

I agreed with him entirely, but this was very much not like him. I set my cup down and reached up to press a hand against his forehead. He didn't feel like he was running a fever, but there was definitely something strange. He batted my hand away.

"What?"

"You want me to go into the forest?"

"What?" he said again, though there was the faint darkness of a blush on his cheeks now. "You love exploring."

"I do," I agree. "And, look, I know you don't mind that I go into the forest, but you've never really encouraged it either."

"Well, no," he agreed, and for a second he looked guilty.

"So you're doing it now because?"

"I just...I thought you could take a radio with you to test if the signal's actually penetrating any distance in this forest. I mean, it is. It must be. I just thought..."

I laughed. Of course, it was something to do with the signal. I didn't even mind. Luke being worried about the signal was normal. I could cope with the normal range of Luke's emotions. I couldn't deal with him completely changing his personality overnight. He looked slightly embarrassed still but didn't stop me when I leaned in and took his face between my hands, kissing him.

We lost a little time that way. I hadn't meant the kiss to turn into anything, but the lightest brush of lips; an expression of how happy I was, how funny he was, and the absurdity of our entire situation. Kissing Luke was never a simple thing, though, and somehow my arms ended up around his neck, his body pressing me back down into my bunk.

He pulled back and looked at me with those big dark eyes of his. He always looked dazed when he pulled away from a kiss, as though he didn't get how it had managed to become so intense.

"Hey," I said, reaching up to brush his cheek.

"Hey."

"Want to maybe skip the forest today and stay in bed instead?"

I didn't think he'd actually go for it, but, to my credit, he did look tempted for a solid few seconds before shaking his head shyly.

"Sorry. I just really want to know the transmitter's actually working."

"Fine, workaholic," I said, though I pressed a kiss to the corner of his lips so he knew I wasn't actually mad. "You're going to have to let me out of bed though or I really am going to try to tempt you to stay in here."

He laughed, but got himself off my bed, which I firmly told myself I wasn't disappointed about. Besides, I was going out into the world, and I had Luke's permission to go as far as I wanted.

It took me a little while to get changed, and when I came out Luke was checking the array. I had this horrible mental image of him sitting there all day, checking it over and over again and not hearing anything back. That was too depressing. I made my way over to where Luke was sitting in the chair next to the receiver and draped myself all over his back.

"Hey," he said, squeezing my arm. "You're ready. Let me get the radio."

"You know, I was thinking," I said into his ear. "Maybe you should come into the forest with me. We could explore together." I thought about showing him my waterfall. The place where I'd thought about building a house. Maybe we'd see some of the more interesting plant and wildlife. Maybe, when he saw the fruit hanging thick on the bushes, we'd look at each other and smile, scoop it up and eat it. I'd done every test I could, and I was as sure as I could be that at least it wouldn't kill us.

"I can't," he said, squeezing my arm. "Not today. If there's someone in range, they should have picked up the signal by now. I'm expecting some kind of reply. I mean, they might not physically be here for a long time but a signal... I need to be here. I can't miss that."

"Oh," I said. Yeah, I could see how he wouldn't want to. He'd rigged the thing, so it broadcast an alarm if it got an incoming signal, which was good as I'd probably wouldn't have got him into bed the night before without it, but there was no way we'd hear that out in the forest.

So much for my daydream.

I let him set me up with a radio before trekking out into the forest.

I spent the first few minutes of my walk feeling sorry for myself, but it was so easy to fall into the beauty of the place and lose myself in the plethora of new life all around me. The entire place was spectacular; I couldn't help but imagine Earth used to be like this. I'd seen photos, of course, but never anything in the flesh. I knew pockets of rainforest still existed, or they did when we left earth. They'd never seemed as vivid or alive as this, though. They'd seemed fragile and breakable, barely hanging on.

Of course, this place was no stronger than they were. I knew that. I knew how quickly humanity could destroy beauty, even when it didn't mean to.

Freed of the need to hold myself back and checking for the signal on the radio every thirty minutes, I followed the river up further than I ever had before. I'd almost expected the fork that linked my two rivers together to be just around the bend, but I walked for two hours before I found the split. The river that led to the waterfall was wider and more powerful, more beautiful. I sat at the edge of it while I ate the sachet of nutrient powder I'd brought with me.

As I rested, I watched the water and it really hit me how indescribably lucky I was. What had happened was terrible, that was undeniable, but if anything had happened even a little differently, I wouldn't have this. I wasn't sure the beauty of the forest was worth the magnitude of what I'd lost, but it was something. Luke's kisses could never completely fill the hole from knowing we were alone forever, but it helped soothe me a little at least. I couldn't regain what I'd lost but there were still these moments, these flickers of hope and joy.

There were still things to live for.

Sunning myself by that alien river on a planet that no human had ever walked on before, I realised I'd be okay. I thought maybe they weren't wrong to put me on the mission. I did have some strength, and I was going to heal.

I sat there for a while and let myself soak in the feeling, soak in the sun. Let my arms relax and my legs. The river was gentle besides me, the insects loud in the trees.

This place could be home. A real home. Not the kind of home I'd ever imagined for myself, but then what in this mission was ever going to match up to something I'd imagined for myself? I was on an alien planet. Even if Eileen had survived, everything would have changed. At least this way I got to direct that change. *We* got to direct that change.

Luke and I had a future here. It might be a fight to get him to realise that, but he would—eventually. We'd be okay.

I finished up my pack of nutrient power and stood, stretched, looked around my kingdom. I wouldn't trade Eileen for this, but since I'd lost her anyway, I was glad this was my reward.

I walked for another hour or so before I was ready for a short rest. I lay in a patch of something that resembled moss and tried to focus on the future until I got bored, then I spent a little more time wandering. It seemed the trees were getting bigger, and the bigger and older then got, the stiffer they were. Some of them could almost be considered woody, their old leaves stiff like boards.

The trees would be perfect for a house, and they made me think of Luke and my little clearing with my waterfall. It would be far enough away that I didn't have to look up at the ship every day, didn't have to think about everyone who died.

Though, maybe that wasn't a good thing. Maybe I should be thinking about the people who'd died. Maybe it was my burden to carry.

It wasn't like Luke would go for building a little cabin, anyway. Not for a long time, if ever. He might be right about that. If someone was out there and they'd pick up the signal, there wouldn't be any point in building a cabin. They might already have found us and be on their way.

That thought was insidious. If they had, everything here was over. Luke would want to go to them or to let them come to us. There'd be no house by the waterfall, no quiet, comfortable life.

Once there, it was the kind of thought that rattled around and around in your head. I wanted to know, though, so I headed back with my mind circling about the idea we'd have received a signal. I knew I should be happy about it. I would be, even if only a little. Life would be more regular.

I wouldn't be sad to leave behind the shadow of the ship full of my friends' bodies. And everything wasn't necessarily lost if we rejoined society. I could still see Luke; we could share a shelter and stick together. Things might even be better. There'd be and friends and community. It had to be better.

I reached the path where I'd broken off to go to the waterfall. It was later than I normally left the forest—though still a way off night—and I hadn't meant to leave the stream. I found myself walking into the trees anyway. I found the waterfall without much effort and stood at the top of it for a while just breathing.

Whatever happened, I'd be okay. Wherever I went, I'd always have my memories. I sat there and internalised every inch of this place. Let myself feel it until I felt like I could close my eyes and it was just there, under my eyelids.

Then I went back to camp.

The sky was starting to darken by the time I left the forest. Luke was sitting where I'd left him, though he must have moved through the day as some of the damage the previous storm had done—which we'd been ignoring as I helped him with the array—was finally cleared away. I walked towards him and he stood to meet me.

"It worked," I offered, waving the radio at him. "As far as I could walk today."

"Yeah?" he said, pleased. "That's great. I mean, I knew it would but-"

I cut him off, desperate to know. "Any signal?"

"No," he said. His expression seemed to droop a little, and I tried not to feel too happy in the face of his sadness. "But it'll come. There has to be someone out there."

"There has to be," I agreed, trying not to look back at the ship. If we were the only ones who survived from our ship, what's to say the same hadn't happened to everyone else?

I didn't want to mention that to Luke, though. Not now.

"I hope you didn't just sit there listening to the radio all day," I said, stepping closer. He reached for me, and I leaned into his chest, the movement almost feeling like second nature by now.

"No," he said, and there was that smile creeping back. I adored how he never managed to stay sad for long. "Actually, I had a little project that I finished. I think you're going to like it. I hope you're going to like it."

"Intriguing," I said, squeezing my arms around him. "Go on, then. Show me."

"I will," he said, stepping back out of my arms.

As much as I'd had time to form any expectation, I'd thought he might lead me towards the ship, show me some other piece of equipment he'd found or some practical thing. He'd been talking about some digging equipment or land clearing things that might help us make a path to the river.

Instead, he took my hand and led me down towards the house. Twilight was falling and I could see the lights inside were already lit. I glanced back at Luke who was smiling at me like he wanted me to go in. I did.

Nothing had changed in the main room, but my eye was drawn through to the bedroom. Something had definitely changed there. The room was now filled with a bed. A double bed, with plenty of space for both me and Luke. We were going to be able to sleep together!

"Go on," he said from behind me. "Try it. I think I've made it stable enough."

"I'm sure you have," I said, crawling onto it. I wasn't going to be able to get at the drawers I'd stashed under our beds, but it'd be worth it to be able to sleep there. The mattress was obviously three jammed in together and they didn't quite fit. He'd unzipped a pile of sleeping bags and laid them out. Though they didn't quite work as sheets, they made the entire thing feel like a nest.

Luke followed me onto the bed, sprawling out over the space that used to be his and was now ours.

"Do you like it?"

"Of course, I do," I said, spreading out so I was next to him, my head resting against his arm. I'd get to sleep like this tonight. No more retreating back to my own bunk when we were finished. We'd get to sleep in each other's arms. He'd be right there when I reached out for him, not across a gap. There'd be no more waking with dead arms hanging over the bed. There.

I loved it.

"I used another bed panel," Luke said, patting it. "I mean, we have spares. I don't know why they didn't design them like this from the outset, though of course they were only meant to be temporary places while we got real building going."

"It's great," I said, twisting around so I could see him. He was beaming down at me, and I was starting to wonder if he always smiled for everyone, or maybe he just always smiled for me. Maybe he just really liked me?

"I'm glad you think so," he said. He shifted, turning to face me so we were curled together like quotation marks, the bed between us. "I mean, I was worried it might be a little bit too much, too pushy. I just... I really wanted to fall asleep with you in my arms."

My heart swelled up like I was the Grinch at Christmas. I reached for him and he moved forward into my arms, sliding a hand onto my hips and the other into my hair as he pressed forward and kissed me deeply and filled with longing. I moaned against his lips and kissed him back, running my fingers through his hair then down his back as I pressed myself against him.

He'd built me a bed. A nest, almost. A safe space for us. Maybe we would be okay. Maybe I meant something to him like he meant something to me. The kind of contentment and longing that I'd felt hours earlier lying in the sun before my doubts and fears started to creep back in, started to bubble up in me again.

Though there were also more practical implications. We'd managed—just about—to do everything two men could do together, or at least everything I felt like trying. There were limitations to being together on a single bed, though. We'd dragged the mattresses out into the common room and tried to use the floor, but it just hadn't felt good. It hadn't felt intimate but rather quick and dirty. Sometimes quick and dirty was exactly what I wanted, but sometimes...

I ran my hand up and down his side, then slid it under his shirt, letting it run against the muscles there. His body was familiar now, after so many nights together. He brought his hand around to mine, grabbing it through the thin fabric of my T-shirt before pulling back.

"Hey," he said, eyes dark and heavy.

I grinned. "So, you just want to use this bed to hold me while I sleep?"

"I mean, are there other uses?"

"God, I hope so," I said, tugging at his shirt.

Laughing, he grabbed my hip and pushed me onto my back, quickly straddling me. I looked up at him, glorious and strong. He smiled and played with the hem of his shirt, then with one quick motion pulled it up over his head. My mouth went dry at the flex of his shoulders, the expanse of skin exposed to me.

He was so fucking hot. I wanted to eat him up. I reached up and grabbed at him, pulling him down on top of me before kissing him again. His weight held me on the bed, crushing me between body and mattress, and I loved it. I pressed myself into him and he just held me down, keeping me right where he wanted me.

For a while, we lay there, kissing and touching, then he moved down and pressed soft kisses along my jaw and down my neck. I arched up into him, gasping and he continued to pressed hot kisses along the neck of my T-shirt, making me want more.

"Move," I said, shoving at him. He pulled back and noticed me squirming to remove my shirt. He reached to help me and, both shirtless now, we fell back onto the bed. My head hit the mattress and my back arch as he returned his mouth to my neck.

It had never been like this before. With past lovers, I'd always been careful to keep a distance. Now, none of that mattered.

Luke left bruising kisses across my chest and my body sang. I raised my hands to run along his arms and shoulders and feel his muscles work. It was so much.

He drew back suddenly, looking down at me with pupils blown wide, and shiny, wet lips. I gasped as he leaned down again and kissed my lips, fucking my mouth with his tongue. I relaxed for him, my eyes falling shut as he covered me completely.

Luke pulled back again. I almost protested but he grabbed my fly, opening my trousers then pulling them down. I wriggled help him but he didn't seem to need it. He seemed entirely focused on me and what he was doing to me. I loved it.

"God," I panted, reaching for him. "This is... this is crazy hot, right? I mean, you're not normally so..."

"Are you saying we normally have boring sex?"

"No," I said quickly, though he didn't look mad. "I just... this is more...right?"

"Do you like it?"

"God, yes," I said, grabbing him by the shoulders and lifting my hips to meet him. I wrapped my arms around his neck, keeping him close while I kissed him. I could never get bored of kissing him and having him so close.

I might have pulled him down on top of me again, but my trousers were only halfway off and I really wanted to be naked with him. I pulled away quickly and freed my legs. I glanced at him and saw him watching me, eyes heavy, before he realised what I was doing and copied me, throwing his trousers to the side of the bed and stripping out of his underwear. Finally, we were both naked.

We met in the middle again, hands clinging and lips finding each other. I grabbed a handful of his gorgeous butt and squeezed. He gasped into my mouth and moved against me. It was awesome.

I wanted him to fuck me. I wanted to fuck him, too. I wanted to touch him all over and be touched, to come in his mouth and his hand and on the planes on his chest but, right then, I wanted him to fuck me.

"Luke," I said, bringing my hands up to tangle his hair. "Tell me you're planning to fuck me."

"If that's what you want..."

"It is everything I want," I said. I found myself pulling his hair a little, tightening my fist without thinking. He gasped, looking at me with wide eyes.

I needed him so much.

"Tell me you put the lube somewhere we can reach."

"Of course," he said, apparently offended I even had to ask. He let go of me to scoot down the bed and I took the chance to grab all our pillows and prop myself up. He'd apparently brought in more pillows when he'd been dabbling in domesticity and I loved it.

He came back with the bottle and a wide-eyed look like he'd been thinking about this all day, and now it was coming true. I reached for him again and pulled him down onto my pillow pile. It took a little shifting to get comfortable but then it was perfect, pressed in there by him.

He kept touching me, hands running down my sides and over my chest. I gasped at his touch and he laughed at my sensitivity, kissing me again and again.

Eventually, I pushed him back. Kissing was nice, but I'd made up my mind about what I wanted and it was something more than that.

"Luke," I said, trying my best to look serious, "come on. We can't just play around all day."

"I mean, at the moment, we probably can," he said, but he did grab the lube. "What do you think about that? We could stay in here all day. We could see how many times we can come in a day? Or we could draw it right out. I could bring you right up to the edge them back down over and over, really make you beg for it."

My cock was definitely interested in that idea, and he was too. He was long and heavy against my hips and it was hard to not just rub against him to try to get him off.

"Maybe I'll do that to you," I said. "Tie you down to the bed all day and not let you come. We could do both of your ideas at the same time. I could have orgasm after orgasm and not let you come at all."

"God," he groaned, drizzling lube onto his fingers. "That'd be hot as fuck."

"Maybe one day," I said, adjusting my position a little to make it easier to get at my ass. "Not today though."

"No, not today," he agreed with a little chortle. He shifted down on the bed to lie between my legs. The position was a little awkward so I put my legs around my shoulder and he didn't stop me. Instead, he leaned forward and started pressing feather light, teasing kisses down my cock. I whimpered, gasped, tried to move against him but I didn't have a lot of purchase. It was easy enough for him to hold me down.

As he kissed me, his other hand slid behind me and found my hole. He brushed over it gently, making sure the entire area was slippery and wet. Then, in one motion, he took the head of my cock into his mouth and pushed a finger into my ass.

I swore, fisted the sheets, and shook with the effort of staying still. He didn't seem to mind, humming around my cock and pulling off again as he worked the finger inside me, moving it around and getting my body used to its width. I lay there and tried to think about relaxing, but it was hard to think about anything at all with the combined heat of his mouth and the pressure at my hole.

He took his mouth off me when he took his finger out, grabbing the lube again then came back. This time he kissed my thighs as he slid two fingers in, and I opened for them easily.

It took a little more lube and a change in the position of his hand but he managed to find my prostate. The soft brush of his fingers against it was maddening, and I started begging, words just tumbling out of my mouth. He laughed against me and carried on stroking me, sending licks of pleasure through my body but it wasn't enough. I needed more.

"Stop," I gasped. "God, stop. I don't want to come on your fingers today. I want you to fuck me."

"Are you sure, babe? You seem to be enjoying this." He curled his fingers inside me again in just the right way to make me mewl.

"Luke."

"But, if you want my cock so badly..."

"Yes," I gasped. He grinned then leaned down to kiss the head of my hard cock, glistening with pre-come. I really wasn't going to last long. His ability to pull an orgasm out of me without even touching my cock was something we'd already established and I was so close, but not close enough.

He adjusted, throwing my legs up over his shoulder and bending me in half. I liked it like this, liked watching his face as he sank into me.

"You ready?" he asked, running lube over his cock with his slick hand. I wondered distantly, if he'd thought to bring across spare sleeping bags for his new bed. It didn't matter. I'd send him for them later it we needed them.

"Do it," I said, and he did. He was thicker and blunter than his fingers. I felt so full. I felt impaled, which I suppose I was. I felt covered, wrapped up in him, completely surrounded by him and part of him.

Then he started to move.

He made a few attempts to find an angle where he was brushing over my prostate, sending curls of pleasure down through me. He was grunting now and it was a good thing we were alone with no one to disturb, because I don't think I could have held in my cries of pleasure, the words falling from my tongue begging him for more. Harder. Deeper.

Then he got his wet hand on my cock and that was it. I was coming. I felt like I was shaking apart and his body...his arms enfolding me...his dick inside me, they were the only things keeping me together. I felt undone.

When I was finished, he pulled out of me slowly, his still hard dick hanging between us for a second. I eyed it.

"You can carry on, if you want." I got overstimulated easily after orgasming, but sometimes that could be good.

"Nah," he said, leaning in to kiss my sweaty cheek, which somehow felt more intimate than anything we'd done before. "Here, let's do this."

Luke moved me onto my side. He ran more lube between my thighs then pushed his cock between them I squeezed a little, made sure it was good and tight for him, then just lay back to feel. He thrust into me, pressing his face into my shoulder. I reached out and found his hand, squeezed it tight, then held on to him until he came, gasping my name and holding tightly to my hand.

We lay there for a while in the post-orgasmic haze, but my thighs soon started to feel sticky as the come dried on then. I tried to stay still for him, for his afterglow, but I ended up sitting up anyway and poking at where I was covered in various fluids. I wrinkled my nose in distaste.

I didn't know how I'd managed to end up with both of our come on me, but next time it'd be his turn.

"Hey," he said, and I turned to see him smiling up at me, come-drunk and stupid. "You're beautiful."

I smiled. "You are, too, honey. Come on, let's get you clean."

He stumbled out of the bed for me and trailed me to the shower. He seemed to wake up a little there. He kissed me as we washed each other, long and sweet. I loved kissing in the wake of an orgasm. It was too early to get really turned on again, so the heat just sat low in my belly like a simmer. Like a promise.

He had brought over spare sleeping bags, so we changed the bed together before crawling in. Sleeping together took a little negotiation but we settled eventually with me as the little spoon, curled much like I normally slept only with Luke along my back, keeping me warm and close.

I held his hand as I drifted into sleep.

Chapter Twenty-One

LIFE TOOK ON a pattern again. It always seemed to, I found. Even in the most ridiculous of circumstances, humans seem to build routines. Luke woke early and went for a jog. I say "went" as though he had a destination, when really, he circled our clearing, but it was a big enough space, and he circled it more than once. I'd wake up and make us food—bland nutrient paste—and we'd eat together before he'd man the radios, and I'd go into the forest.

Most mornings, at first, I tried to get him to come with me. He'd always look sad and look back at the radios like they might be upset if he left them. I knew, really, he was worried. He'd expected to hear something in the first few days and every day after that, the air seemed to get a little thicker.

I came back for lunch, which we ate together, then we'd do something together. Sometimes we explored the outskirts of our clearing. We cut down one of the trees and found that at its core there was an almost solid stem, good for building. Luke, as it turned out, knew a thing or two about carving, so he made a few things. Small statues, at first. After a while, he set to work on a chair. I didn't stop him. The chairs we'd brought with us were flimsy and uncomfortable, designed more for ease of storage than anything. The plan had always been for them to be temporary.

I tended my experiments, which kept right on being good. I thought about pushing Luke to eat the native food but he always dodged the conversation.

We'd have sex in the evenings. Sometimes in the afternoon. Some afternoons that was all we did. We never quite reached the day-long sex marathons we talked about, Luke had to go out and worry at the communications array and I found myself out in the forest, but we managed some pretty respectable afternoons. Most days we ended tucked together, sated, in our little nest.

Maybe it wasn't the life I'd imagined while lying in the sun on that rock. The ship was still there always, the bodies still frozen inside it, waiting. There was no little cabin, no lake, no long swims by the waterfall. But it was a life, and not a bad one at that. We were together. I explored. Luke waited.

The array didn't chime.

Chapter Twenty-Two

IT WAS AFTERNOON. A glorious day, like they all were. That morning, I'd bathed in the river. I'd only meant to wade but when I got in there, the water felt so good on my skin, so I'd stripped down. It was just deep enough to submerge myself, to let the water run all over my body. It felt good. Made me feel alive.

Heading back to camp, it felt like the further I went, the more my feet dragged. I kept on anyway. I had to go back, where else was I going to go?

Like most days, Luke was in the clearing crouched over the array. It didn't seem to be enough to know it'd chime if we got a response anymore; he needed to be right there looking at it.

I let him be and went into the house to make our lunch. I carried it out to him and he'd barely grunted as it set it down next to him.

"Luke," I said softly, "come on, you need to eat."

"I will," he said, fingers hovering over the dials, like he hadn't checked them all a million times already. "I'm just waiting."

"Sure," I said, though he wasn't just waiting. "But, you know this stuff is pretty vile, and it only gets worse if you let it go cold. You're going to end up with a nutrient powder brick again."

He snorted, but he took the cup I was holding out to him, even if he didn't look away from his instruments. I took it as a victory and backed away.

Sometimes with Luke, the only thing to do was back away and try again later.

I spent a few minutes sitting beside him, eating in silence. I contemplated how hard it would be to drag him from his focus and get him to do something else. I'd had some success before with tasks that needed doing around the camp and even more success with sex. It felt, though, like it was getting to be a more and more common thing, having to drag him away from his work. I kind of hated it.

Instead, I took myself back into the house. Alien planet or not, there were things to do. We hadn't bothered with laundry—we had an entire ship's worth of things to go through—but I dragged all our dirty linens and clothes out anyway and took them back to the ship. We'd started using a small store room for them and I stood in the doorway looking at the piles of laundry. Our supplies weren't going to last forever; we might have to wash some of this eventually. I suspected some of the sleeping bags were beyond saving. They'd been left for too long and they were too messy, but most of them should wash.

Luke probably wouldn't like it, though. He didn't like anything that implied that our stay here might be more than the most temporary of things. I got that, I did, but at the same time, the longer we left some of this, the worse it was going to get, and I didn't want to have to try to replace them or make my own.

Still, it wasn't a problem I needed to deal with right then, so I grabbed new clothes and new linen and went back to restock the shelter. I changed the bed, did the washing up, and cleaned the bathroom. We were both neat, clean people. We'd been raised that way by the programme.

I headed back out into the idyllic sunshine. The planet remained beautiful. The spaceship continued to loom ominously above us. Luke still wouldn't move from the array.

I went over to him and sat down, taking his hand. He looked at me this time, at least, and smiled. But his eyes drifted back to the console.

"You know," I said slowly. Tempting him away was a delicate game. "They probably received the signal and just haven't had time to mount a rescue yet. Running a colony must be a full-time job."

They'd have pinged us. That was the protocol. Even if they couldn't come, they should have sent a signal back. But this game hinged on us both carefully ignoring that. "Right," Luke said, as if he had something to prove. "I mean, they might not even be anywhere near us. It'll take them a while to get here."

If they weren't close, I doubt they'd be coming. "The forest's so thick; they could be only a few metres away before we knew about them."

"That's right," Luke agreed, eyes scanning the clearing as though he expected them to emerge at any second. Slowly, his gaze drifted to the mountain. "They'll probably be here any time."

"Right," I agreed. Because the other possibility couldn't be spoken. "Anyway, I was wondering if you maybe wanted to do something. Like, I'm really ready for you to get done making that chair."

"Our chairs are kind of terrible," he said, relaxing a fraction. He had to know as much as I did that this was all bullshit, everything we'd said meant nothing, but it let him buy a few more minutes of the fantasy we'd created together. "But, aren't there better things we could be doing with our time?" His eyes drifted to my mouth and my heart quickened. I licked my lips a little and he followed the motion.

"I could be convinced."

He smiled.

Chapter Twenty-Three

WEEKS PASSED.

Chapter Twenty-Four

THE SUN WAS lower in the sky than I expected when I came out of the forest. I blinked at it, taking it in. Damn.

It wasn't so bad. There were only the merest hints of twilight, but there shouldn't have been any twilight at all. I should have come back at lunch time. I must have been distracted.

Luke sat at the radio, of course. He looked tired, which was pretty rich as he never seemed to do anything anymore—just wait.

At least he sat in one of the chairs he'd made himself now. We each had one and they maybe weren't the most comfortable things I'd ever sat on, but they were more than sturdy enough and we'd cannibalised some pillows to make cushions. Mine was outside the shelter so I could sit on it in the evening and watch the sun. Luke's was by the radio.

I went back to the hut first and checked the time. It was only about dinner time. Days were getting shorter, which wasn't unexpected but, still, there was so much about this planet we didn't know yet.

I'd mentioned our lack of knowledge of the planet to Luke once and he'd stopped talking to me and walked away. I didn't know if he was just scared about what was to come or he didn't want to admit to himself how little knowledge we'd been sent with, how much of a gamble this entire mission was and how it made it so unlikely anyone else had survived, given what a botched job it all was.

He was doing that a lot, too.

I grabbed a few nutrient pouches and made them up. I made myself choke mine down in the shelter. I couldn't carry on eating like this.

I grabbed the other cup. Luke didn't even look up when I approached.

"Hey," I said, setting the cup down beside him on him table.

He snorted.

"I made this up for you. Come on, you've gotta eat."

"Wondered if you were going to bother coming back today."

"Of course, I was going to come back," I said, rolling my eyes. Where else would I sleep? Who else would I talk to? Things might be a little frosty between us but they weren't that bad.

He took the cup and started eating it mechanically.

"You know," I said, watching his jaw clench, "I'm sure the native plants are good to eat. We could just try some. I mean, they might not taste great, I don't even know, but..."

"Alex."

I stopped talking.

He picked at his food, I cast about for something to talk about. Anything would do.

I used to think Luke was easy to talk to.

Maybe I should just go. He'd crawl into bed with me eventually. Maybe not sleep. Sometimes I woke up through the night and he wasn't there. There were dark rings under his eyes, evident even against his soft brown skin. I wanted to sooth them away.

"So," I said, eyes falling on the silent radio. "I guess they didn't get the signal yet. I mean, the other ships could be on the other side of the planet for all we know."

"Alex."

I stopped talking.

There was something pained in the set of his jaw. The beginning of an acceptance that maybe this would be it. Maybe it'd be him and me here together and nobody else coming.

Maybe we'd never see anyone else again. Maybe humanity died here with us. The hopes of humanity might amount to so much space debris.

I felt sick.

"I'm going to go lie down," I said, standing up.

He nodded, stiff and mechanical.

I turned to the shelter, took a few steps, then stopped myself. I turned and went back to him then leaned down and gently pressed one quick kiss to his cheek.

Then I went to lie in bed.

The thing was, I had already accepted us being alone. I'd planned out the cabin we could build by my waterfall. I'd considered what we were eventually going to have to do with the ship full of bodies, I couldn't stand the thought of leaving them there to rot in the ship that was meant to keep them safe. I'd been thinking about crops and planting and if it was even a thing we should do.

I just couldn't accept Luke like this, and I didn't know how to make him see that. I could do this, it'd hurt, but I could live here, but I couldn't do it alone.

I needed Luke to not make me do it alone.

He crawled into bed hours after me. He kissed apologies into the skin of my neck, and I held him and wished he meant it.

Chapter Twenty-Five

THE MORNING OF the storm, we didn't even really worry. The sky was heavy and dark but we'd lived through a few storms. Everything looked terrible. There'd been some wind, but it was never that bad. There was normally just lots of rain, like the planet stored it all up to have a good downpour every so often.

We went about our day as usual. Luke was already by the radio. He'd taken to varying the signal and to jumping between frequencies, both transmitting and listening. At least it was better than sitting there and doing nothing.

I went into the forest. I didn't want to go far, not as far as I had been going, so I went to my waterfall. I sat there next to it, looking down. I wished I was brave enough to dangle my legs over the edge, but I knew, if I did, I might fall and Luke might not notice for hours. I could die there and leave him alone. I'd never do that.

I went back earlier than I had been doing. I didn't let myself get caught up. Not after what happened last time, though, I doubted Luke would follow me again. If he did, my frequent trips had worn a path through the vegetation to my clearing.

He'd still never seen my clearing, though, he'd heard me talk about it. He wouldn't leave the radio.

I got back in good time, made lunch, and took anything I thought might be damaged inside. I stood and watched the mountain for a while. It seemed like it was already raining over there. I wondered, idly, how long it'd take me to walk there. If Luke would even let me. If Luke would even notice I was gone.

Probably best not to ask.

It got dark early and Luke left the radio on his own, checking it was all covered in waterproof tarpaulin and safe under his gazebo. We shared cups of nutrient paste and curled into bed.

I wrapped myself around him and tried not to think.

Chapter Twenty-Six

I WOKE UP to an unnatural pounding against the shelter, a screech like something being torn, and a strong hand wrapped around my arm. I pulled back, flailing and blinking my eyes open. The bedroom light was lit and I could see through to the living room, see the roof straining. I could see what looked like a solid wall of water outside the door we'd naively left open. I'd moved my beautiful chair inside, but it was soaked anyway.

Luke was looking at me, eyes wide. He reached for me again, grabbed my arm a little too tight. He screamed something, but I couldn't hear it over the rain.

The house shuddered, and I pulled my legs up to my chest. This was bad. This was so very bad.

Luke pulled at my arm, and I scooted closer to him. He looked... happy, alive. Not what I'd been expecting. He wrapped his arms around me and I buried myself in him.

The house shrieked again. The wind seemed to be getting in somehow, which it hadn't been before. I pressed into Luke's side. These things weren't meant to last forever, but surely, they should stand this. They shouldn't be groaning like this.

It creaked again. Then, slowly, a corner seemed to give. It buckled, pushed back on itself to create a hole in the roof. Water came gushing through, immediately soaking my table.

It was destroying my house.

"Luke," I screamed, though, I didn't think he'd be able to hear me over the rain. The roof gave another lurch and slowly began to peel back; the wind, a giant hand rolling it away and letting the rain in.

It was going to ruin everything. My chair, my plumbing, my bed. Everything we'd built here.

We weren't safe.

"We have to go," I yelled, not even able to hear my own words, and scrambled towards the end of the bed. Luke must have realised what I was doing because he scrambled with me, grabbing my hand as I slid off the bed, just as the roof rolled back and dumped a torrent onto me.

For a second, I stood there, fighting just to breathe with the shock of if, the pressure of it. Then Luke was walking forward, pulling me by our joined hands, and I didn't have any choice but to follow him.

There was no time to find one of the handheld torches, so we fumbled in the dark. There was no light from the small distant moons. The clouds were too thick. Not even a single star shone through. I clung to Luke, stumbling as the winds buffeted me and the mud under my feet seemed to give way with every step.

I pressed as close to Luke as I could, limbs straining. If I lost him in this, how was I going to find him again? I'd be alone.

I couldn't let go.

He pulled and I followed. I didn't even know where he was trying to head. The forest would help, though it was far from perfect as we'd learnt last time. Perhaps he'd lead us to the ship?

I did not want to go to the ship, but even I could admit it was probably the best place to be.

I stepped on something, something sharp, and pulled my foot back right away, swearing and cursing, but the movement overbalanced me. My remaining foot was in a slurry of mud, not on firm ground. It slid. I fell.

My hand was pulled from Luke's. For a second, I was there in the dark, alone, hands grasping out for him, screaming, my body aching, the water pushing me down.

Then he was there, awkward hands grasping my elbows, sliding up to my wrists. He yanked me up, wrapped his arms around me, and for a second we just stood there.

We were alive, so alive. I wanted to stay that way. I didn't want this to be how humanity ended.

Slowly, carefully, we edged our way forward. We shuffled, clinging to each other for support. Now my eyes were adjusting, I thought I saw shapes, not anything distinct. Nothing I could navigate by.

Suddenly, the rain was lighter. The wind still pushed at us but the weight of the water was gone and I stood there gasping.

Above me, the sound of the rain hit the metal. We were under the ship.

Oh, god, I didn't want to die under the ship.

Luke pulled back from me a little and stumbled forward. I followed him, pressing my body against his. It was drier, but the wind still drove some rain to us, and the floor was still soaked.

Then Luke pulled me forward, shoved me in front of him and I grasped for something, my hands closing around a metal bar.

It was the ladder. Luke had found the ladder we'd left under the ship. It had been protected enough to still be standing. I climbed slowly, my mud-encrusted hands and feet uncertain on the rungs, then pulled myself into the ship.

I lay there on the floor next to the entrance, breathing. Here, hidden in the ship's belly, the rain was far enough away that I could hear my own laboured breath, the proof of my own existence.

Luke didn't lie in the floor like me. He scrambled up and a second later the room was flooded with light.

I looked down at myself, smeared in mud, then back to him. He looked as bad as me, though he hadn't fallen over in the stuff, and he was still grinning. It was almost manic.

"Luke?"

"Did you hear it?"

"The storm?" I asked, though that absolutely couldn't be what he meant. It was the only thing I'd heard out there.

He snorted, then he grabbed the lamp and started to the ladder again. I blinked at him, agog. He couldn't be going back out there. That was ridiculous.

"What are you doing?" I asked, trying to get in front of him.

"The radio," he said, as though that made sense. "I heard it pinging."

"Luke..."

"It was in the storm, but I heard it. It had to be that."

"It couldn't be that. It's deafening out there, Luke. Even if it had gone off you'd never have heard it."

"I know what I heard."

"Luke..."

"I need to see." He shoved past and left me scrambling. I darted over to where he'd got the lamp from and found another and turned it on. It bathed my empty space in an eerie light. My little room at the bottom of a tomb.

He'd gone mad. Luke had gone mad. Or something like it. He couldn't have heard anything. It wasn't loud enough to hear in the forest; therefore, how could he hear it over the rain?

But, whatever he thought he'd heard, he was out there alone. I couldn't let him be out there alone.

I scrambled down the ladder, the rungs even more treacherous now with left over mud. I could see Luke's lantern bobbing in the distance. My heart was racing, breath coming in pants. The wind was throwing the lantern light everywhere, and the rain was too thick to see through, but he was there.

He was there and he might need me. He couldn't stay out in this.

The lamp fell to the ground.

I started running.

My feet slid in the mud but somehow I kept going forward. The rain pounded on me but I pushed it to the back of my mind. I needed to reach him.

I needed him.

I realised, even before I crashed into his kneeling body, what was wrong. The array. There was so much scattered debris, it was completely irretrievable. I dropped to my knees beside him and he was cradling a piece in his hands. It was caked with mud and bent with electrical components torn from it.

It was over. He wasn't going to be able to build the array again, not like this. The last little hope of us ever being rescued died in me.

Then there was an ominous groaning behind us. There was a thunking sound that could have been my roof coming free. God, if the roof hit us in these winds, that'd be it.

I didn't try to talk, I just leaned in and took Luke's hands. He looked up at me with his big, lost brown eyes and I kissed him with just the barest brush of lips. Then I tugged at him again.

Luke let me help him to his feet. He took the lantern when I pressed it into his hands. He stood when I urged him and pressed against me as we stumbled back into the protection of the ship.

This time, I sent him up the ladder first. I watched his hands shake as he climbed and his feet slipped. It seemed surreal. All this time, he'd been the certain one. He'd been the one with the plan. Luke couldn't be weak. He couldn't be failing here in front of me.

As soon as there was space, I went up the ladder after him. He was waiting for me, and then reached for me, his hands catching in my clothes. He pulled me in, pressed his face into my neck and held me.

I realised the shaking in his shoulders was tears. He was crying. Crying and clinging to me and I didn't know what to do, how to help. I wrapped my arms around him and shushed him. As I stroked his back, I pressed kisses to his hair and his forehead.

Outside, the thunder rumbled. I clung to Luke, pressed my face into him and hoped we'd survive.

Chapter Twenty-Seven

THE NEXT MORNING, I woke up to find Luke already awake, lying there next to me. He looked at me silently, didn't move when I leaned over to brush a kiss across his nose.

"Hey," I whispered, reaching a hand to brush his hair. "We survived the storm."

Luke nodded, but his face stayed passive.

I'd thought that last few weeks had been bad. Luke becoming increasingly disenchanted and the strain between us. I knew instantly this was worse. This wasn't disenchantment; this was Luke leaving me alone here.

I couldn't let him. I didn't know how to stop him, but I couldn't let him just drift away.

The night before, I'd made an effort to get us both clean and changed our clothes, but there'd been so much mud, so much water. I thought briefly about taking us upstairs to the shower we'd used when we'd first got here, but I didn't want to go any further into the ship, not even now, when it'd saved us.

I wanted to go back into the forest to look at the rivers and see how far their banks had swollen. It'd be important information when it came to deciding where to build a house. I was more and more certain I didn't want to build in the clearing with the ship.

I sat up, stretching, and Luke's eyes tracked me. His face stayed horribly neutral.

"Okay," I said, trying to sound cheerful. "Let's get out there and see what needs to be done."

Luke blinked at me. For a second, I thought he was just going to carry on lying there, but then very slowly he sat up. He winced, rolling his shoulders. He blinked again like he was powering up.

"I don't think there's anything to save," he said, and I couldn't help but wonder if he just meant out of our camp or if he meant it in a more existential way.

"Well, we'll never know for sure if we don't go look. Come on."

Luke nodded, though he still looked blank, then pushed himself to his feet. I bit my lip as I watched him. He seemed too stiff, slow. I'd never seen him like this. He was always such a presence defined by his movements.

I went down the ladder first, only because I was worried Luke would just stop halfway down. It gave me a few seconds alone to look out.

The gazebo that had been over the array was smashed into pieces and scattered all the way over to the tree line. Everything that had been in it was now just so much debris, and it was going to take ages to clean up. The array was in pieces. Some of them were sunk in the mud. My little shelter had been peeled like a tin of beans, but the walls were still standing and, from this distance, I couldn't see any obvious damage to the plumbing connecting it to the river, so that might still be working. We could replace the roof. It could be worse.

Luke walked past me, more focused now he was out of the ship and had something to do. He went to the array and knelt and gathered a few pieces into his hands. I followed him.

What could I even say? What can you say to someone whose last hope of ever seeing another person was lying in fragments on the floor? I felt my heart break a little to see it, but in a way, I'd been preparing for this for a long time. I'd never believed we'd be rescued like he did. Maybe I should have tried to prepare him for this, to argue with him. Maybe I should have forced him to climb the ship with me and look out, see that nobody was coming. I'd just wanted his hope. Needed it to give me a reason to get up in the morning when I hadn't had one of my own.

He sat back, eyes vacant, scanning the horizon. Finally, he said softly, "I heard the alarm."

"Honey, it was so loud. You couldn't have."

"I did. I wouldn't lie."

"I don't think you lying." It was true. I thought he believed he'd heard the alarm. I thought he was wrong, but I was sure that was what he believed.

"You think I'm mad."

"I think you were just waking up. I think you heard something but, babe, it wasn't the alarm. It couldn't be. And, hey, if it was, they're on their way, right? It doesn't matter that the array went down?"

"Right," Luke said, though he didn't look convinced. He stood and moved around the area, picking pieces up, and then dropping them. I could see his fingers shaking and my heart ached. I stepped in, grabbed his hands and pressed them to my chest.

"It's going to be okay. Luke, it's going to be okay."

"Because they're coming."

"Even if they're not." I couldn't have said that the day before, but standing in the wreck of the lives we'd built so far, I had to. "We'll find a way, Luke. Me and you."

He nodded, but he wasn't listening. His eyes were far away, scanning the forest. Then he stopped.

"The mountain."

"What?" I asked, turning to look at it. It looked fine, standing there as it usually did. It didn't look like the storm had done it any harm.

"We need to climb it."

"Luke..."

"No, listen, I need to know. I'm sure I heard... but say you're right? Say they're not coming. I need to know. If we climb that, we'll be able to see for miles. We'll know where they are."

Well, we'd certainly get a better view from up there than I had from the ship. Luke had always been the go big or go home type.

"I don't know," I said, biting down on the part of me that wanted to say yes, pull him into the forest and never come out again. "It's a long way, Luke. It might be dangerous. I've been a little way into the forest but I've never been that far. It's really easy to get lost in there."

"We'll follow the river," he said, life seeping back into his cheeks. "It'll end up there eventually, right. That's how rivers work."

"Right," I agreed, nodding helplessly. At least I'd get to see how swollen the rivers were.

"And you keep trying to drag me out there. Come on, it'll be an adventure."

I couldn't say no.

Chapter Twenty-Eight

IT TOOK US a day to be ready to set out. I insisted on putting a new roof on the shelter first, though it wasn't like the insides could be more damaged. It just felt wrong to leave it there skinned, and Luke apparently wanted to keep me calm enough that he agreed to it. We both got a new set of boots. We found some packs meant for the people on our little colony who were meant to go out exploring and we loaded them up with food, spare socks, and some insulated blankets.

We checked around the camp and tidied what we could. It wasn't good to leave it in a mess, even if we were magically picked up by other people. And I didn't want to have to come back and start tidying after we'd climbed a mountain.

There was no specific mountain climbing equipment on the ship but at least we found ropes. I packed a small camping stove so we'd be able to heat out water along with some small water treatment tabs like the ones we used to purify our normal drinking water.

A lot of time was spent making sure a rescue team would know where to look for us if they arrived and we were gone. We wrote notes with our plans and left one of them in the house, another in the ship, another pinned out in the ground with the remains of the communication array as though to yell yes, it is us you're looking for. It was probably excessive, but Luke's shoulders seemed to relax a little with every note we left.

We slept one night inside the ship again. I tried to convince Luke we could sleep in our bed, that it would be better to sleep in our bed, but he didn't think there was any point in it. We'd have to clean everything and drag new mattresses and sleeping bags out there. Instead, we built a kind of nest on the floor of the storage area. Luke slept, while I lay awake and felt all the bodies pressing down above me.

The next morning, we shouldered out packs and set out into the forest.

Chapter Twenty-Nine

"YOU'RE SURE THIS is the quickest way?"

"Yes," I said, leading Luke down the path I'd trodden into the foliage. I wasn't even lying. The branch of the river closest to our landing site meandered before joining up with the branch coming from the waterfall. It made much more sense to cut through the forest there where getting lost wasn't likely.

Luke nodded, but he was worrying his lip. Maybe it wasn't the way we'd written we'd go in our notes – that we'd walk straight upriver – but if we continued on we'd be beyond the point where the two rivers split in a few hours and people weren't going to arrive before then.

They weren't going to arrive at all, of course, but it still felt vaguely disloyal to even think that. Instead, I focused on the path. It was nice to feel like I had a purpose for once, like I was contributing. I wanted to show Luke that my hours spent out here hadn't been a waste and to finally show Luke the clearing.

I made myself not think about that. Made myself just focus on my feet. Whatever idiot ideas I was nursing about what might happen when we walked out into that clearing, they weren't important. They weren't even a thing I needed to think about. Still, they fluttered around the edge of my mind.

We were getting close. I slowed my steps a little. Obediently, Luke followed. I had to let go. I had to not expect anything. Just because I thought it was beautiful. Just because I could imagine building a house there, living there...

Luke wasn't even going to consider it. Luke wanted to go. He wanted other people and that made sense. I wanted other people too. I just...

The trees thinned. I bit my lip, forced my feet to keep going. He wasn't going to react like I wanted, and it was okay. We were just going to keep walking. At least I'd get to see it one more time. At least I'd get to know.

We stepped out of the trees.

The open area to the river was clear. It wasn't flooded, anyway. The river was high, pushing at its banks, the water dirtier with silt and quicker than I was used to, but it wasn't flooded. We could build a home here and not be flooded.

Not that Luke would but...

I walked over to the edge of the cliff so I could see the ground below. The lake had risen significantly so we wouldn't be able to build down there. It wouldn't matter, though, as long as there was one place we could build.

I risked a glance back at Luke. He was looking at me. He wasn't frowning, at least. His face was oddly flat. That probably wasn't good. I'd wanted...well, what I'd wanted didn't matter. I'd known I wasn't going to get it. This was my place, not his. He wouldn't care for it like I did.

"This is your waterfall?" he asked uncertain.

"Yes." I smiled at him, and he nodded. Message acknowledged, even if it hadn't really been processed.

For a minute, I considered making a case for it. It wouldn't be a bad life here. It'd be quiet, at least and perhaps a little lonely, but we'd have each other and that was something. We could have a home. We could have a life. We could be together. If I was wrong, if Luke had heard something on the radio, they wouldn't find us any quicker if we climbed the mountain. We could just settle down here, and if someone came, they came. If not...

Luke's eyes were already fixed on the mountain though. He had to know. I knew he did.

And what kind of life could we have, after all, with him always having one eye on the horizon? Always waiting for rescue?

We had to go.

"Right," I said, turning my back on the waterfall. "Let's do this thing."

Chapter Thirty

THERE WAS A thrill in leaving the places I knew behind. I'd explored as far as I could go in half-day's walk pretty well, but obviously I'd never been beyond that. I wouldn't have left Luke. Now, with him by my side, I could carry on. I didn't have to worry about going back, and it was freeing and terrifying

I stopped at the tree that marked the edge of what I knew and put my hand on it. I'd literally marked it, tying a blue rope around it like a barrier, something to remind me to turn back, to tie me to the clearing and to Luke and to the ship and responsibility. I didn't have to worry about that now. For all that was terrible about this situation, there was a strange joy curling in my gut too.

"Alex?"

I turned and looked. Luke had made it further down the river, and he was looking back at me, watching my hand on the tree like he wasn't sure what I was doing and expected some kind of arcane magic.

"Sorry," I said, dropping my hand and hurrying to catch him. "Sorry. This is just the furthest I've been."

"Is it?" Luke asked, clearly surprised. "So, from here on out, it's all new to you."

"All new to us both," I agreed. He nodded, then he reached for me, and it was easy to reach back, to let him slide his fingers between mine. It felt good to be touching him, normal. For a second, I could forget he was only out here because his entire world and been thrown off his axis and imagine he was adventuring with me.

"You know, when I first signed up for this, I wanted to be on an exploration team."

"But you're science, right?" Luke asked, frowning.

"Biology, yes. But I wanted...well, it's probably silly. I just always romanticised the idea of heading out into the unknown. I'd always dreamt of making my way through dangerous terrain, testing my ability to survive, walking on ground nobody has walked on before and seeing something new, something so novel it'd shock me. When we were kids, Eileen and I, we used to play at explorer. We used to go out into the park and pretend we were in the desert of the forest. When they started the recruitment drive for this..."

"I bet you were first in line," Luke said, smiling softly.

"Well, if not first, then a close second. My mum didn't like it. We'd lost my dad not long before and she didn't want me to go but...well, I wanted to. When they actually opened general application instead of plucking people from private schools it seemed too good to not at least try."

"Then how did you end up in science?"

A beetle flitted by that I was sure I hadn't seen before. Normally, I'd have stopped, knelt down and taken out a notebook to record it. The urge was there, tugging at me, but Luke's fingers through mine were tugging at me more. I needed to keep moving. I had no idea how long it was going to take us to get to the mountain, but I knew the sooner we got there, the sooner we'd come back.

"Capability."

"You seem pretty capable to me," Luke said, amused. I supposed I would since I'd been the one who was out here every day.

"Not the kind of capability they wanted. I'm not even sure why. Maybe they wanted someone who laughed at danger or someone who could crash through a forest without thinking about the possibility of preserving the local ecosystems. I'm good at biology anyway. I know my way around a lab and I know more than enough to tell you the local fruits are safe, no matter what you think."

"I believe you," he said, squeezing my hand. "It's just... I mean, they're alien. We can't know."

"We can't know anything about this place," I said, waving my hand. It was entirely possible the berries would hold no nutritional value for us but, at this point, I'd take flavour. If they gave me a sensation in my mouth that wasn't chalk, I'd be ecstatic.

"We can't," Luke slowly, softly agreed. "You know, I kind of admire you. Coming out here. I can't... I look at this planet and I just think about all the things it isn't. I think about the careful plan we had and all the reasons it can never work now, about how we've come so far and it's all going to mean nothing."

"I honestly try not to think about it," I said, leaning against him, letting our shoulders bump as we walked. It was a touch uncomfortable maybe, but it was worth it to reassure him I was there with him. "I mean, maybe that's why I walk. All that stuff, that's what I think about when I look at the ship. Out here, I can be an explorer. I can put everything else aside for a bit."

"I'll never make an explorer." He sounded wistful. "It's not a bad thing. I just... I'll just never make an explorer."

"What do you think you would have done if we weren't here?"

"Well, died on Earth?"

"No," I say, waving my hand to dismiss it. "What if you'd lived, say, a few hundred years ago before we destroyed the atmosphere and before the flu pandemics? What would you have been?"

"You know," Luke said, slowly, "I haven't ever thought about that. I guess I've always liked people; maybe some kind of manager. I mean, I never got a choice. I was always going to be a leader. I was always going to manage people. But if I could do anything...what would you do? You can't say explorer."

"I wouldn't," I protested. "I'd be a teacher, I think."

"You could have been a teacher now."

"Not if I wanted to leave the planet. But I think I'd have liked it, teaching. I was always good with kids and, well..." I stopped myself. I was trying very hard not to think about kids. They'd be impossible now, of course.

"Hey," Luke said, squeezing my hand. "We're not alone. I don't care about the array, we're not alone. This isn't how humanity ends."

I pulled my fingers out of his. A few days ago, I might have let myself take comfort in him, at least, believing it. Now I couldn't. Now it was just empty. Empty words meaning nothing. Why should I even listen to him?

I'd never have a family. I'd never have kids. Neither would he. This was how humanity ended, and maybe that was for the best. We'd destroyed one planet, maybe it was good that we'd be stopped before we destroyed another.

"Alex..."

"Come on," I said, picking up my pace. "We've got a lot of ground to cover."

I walked on ahead. He didn't stop me.

Chapter Thirty-One

THAT FIRST NIGHT, we slept in each other's arms. The second night, too, and the third. We talked. We reached for each other. By the end of the first week, we didn't. Not in the same way. Neither of us were exactly used to the exercise, the pods had taken their toll, which was a convenient excuse for our slow drifting apart, our falling into sleep without talking, but the truth of it was every time he insisted help was coming something inside me hurt, and I guessed my obvious belief that nobody was coming did the same to him.

The forest was beautiful, at least, but even I couldn't be interested in it all day every day. It wore on me. It wore on us both.

By the middle of the second week, we were sleeping apart. Luke wasn't talking. I wasn't reaching for his hand.

At the end of week two, on the day we finally lost the tree cover, it started to rain.

By then, we'd walked far enough that my feet were aching, my legs were aching, my back was aching. In fact, it would probably be fair to say my entire body had just been replaced with one big ache. I stepped out of the tree line to see an expanse of rock and scrubland in front of me, watching it curve up into the air, to a mountain Luke expected me to climb. I was done. I'd have been done even without the rain. It was that soft, pervasive rain. The kind that doesn't seem too bad until you've been out in it for an hour and you realise, somehow, it's seeped through all your layers to your skin and you're never going to feel dry again.

I took a few steps back under the shade then sat down heavily. I was probably crushing unique and beautiful wildlife. I didn't care anymore.

Luke carried on. I watched him go, my head down and shoulders hunched. I wondered absently how far he'd get before he'd notice my absence, then I focused on rubbing my ankles instead, trying to get the circulation back into them. I'd slept in my boots for the last two nights, hadn't dared to take them off in case I couldn't get them back on again.

I knew that was probably a stupid idea. I didn't care. We'd never planned for a trek like that. Setting out, I'd thought it'd only take a week tops. We had nutrient packs for three. Now, we were two weeks in.

The river twisted more than we'd expected. Or we'd gone further. When we got halfway through the food, I'd expected Luke to give up and admit it'd been a bad idea and to finally let us go back. Instead, he seemed to have doubled down. We shared a pouch instead of each eating one.

I was cold, wet, hungry, tired, and in pain.

I was done.

I knew Luke thought he needed this. I knew he thought he needed to see. But I had needs too. I was sick of trailing after him.

He stopped out there in the wilderness. He hadn't shaved since we'd left camp, and he looked like a wild man: overgrown and covered in mud. There was something dangerous in his eyes, it seemed, when he let me close enough to see. Like every day brought him a little bit closer to some edge.

He turned, scanned back for me. I waved and he gestured for me to go to him. I shook my head, but he was too far to see. He gestured again, and I held up my arms, making a cross mark above my head.

No.

He started walking back, I turned back to my ankles. I wasn't going on. I was going to rest. I needed at least one day to rest.

"Alex," he shouted, his voice echoing. Somehow, it made the world seem even emptier. I ignored him. I wasn't having this conversation over distance. I pushed back further instead so I could lean against the trunk of the tree. I crossed my ankles. They throbbed quietly back at me.

"Alex," Luke shouted again, a lot nearer this time. I looked up to see he was probably in talking range. He was also soaked. His hair was plastered to his head. His shirt was stuck to him. He was going to take forever to dry out.

I wasn't going to go out there. I wasn't. It was all pointless. Nobody was coming.

"Hey," he said, close enough not to be yelling now. "What's wrong?"

"It's raining," I said. This should be enough. The contemptuous curl of his frown told me he didn't think it was.

"Come on, Alex. If we set a good pace, I think we can be at the real climb by nightfall. We could be at the peak tomorrow night."

"Or, we could stay here," I said in what I hoped was my reasonable voice.

"Alex..."

"No, I'm serious. We could just stay here. We can't walk in that. It's...well...it's not dry under cover, but it's drier. We could rest. You know we need to rest. We've been pushing on for weeks. I don't think there's a muscle in my body that doesn't ache right now."

Luke turned and looked up at the mountain. For a second, he sagged under his load. His hands slackened on the straps of his backpack, his shoulders slumped. He had to know this was crazy. He had to know there was no point in going up there. There was nothing up there we couldn't see down here. We needed to rest. We needed to regroup.

"Please, Luke," I said. I leaned forward, snagging one of his hands. He looked down at our joined hands and blinked. The first few days, we'd held hands a lot. The first few days had been an adventure.

His fingers slid out of mine. He didn't make any attempt to take my hand again. He looked back up at the mountain.

He wasn't going to stop.

"Luke..."

"I have to go," he said. There was a waver in his voice. "I have to... you don't understand."

"No," I agreed. "I don't. Help me to understand, Luke."

"I have to know..."

"I think you already know," I snapped. He flinched.

"But, I need to see. They could be out there. They could be just a little further away. Maybe something went wrong with our signal. Maybe there's a problem with their equipment. If I could just see..."

"Nobody's coming. We're alone"

"You don't know that."

"I do." I only realised once the words were out that I'd yelled them. I'd meant to be calm, measured, but nothing about this was calm, not really. "I do, Luke. Nobody's coming. We are alone, and I'm so fucking tired. I know you can't cope with this. I can't really cope with this, either, but we have to try. Luke, please."

"You don't know that," he said, shaking his head. He was turning back to the mountain. "I have to know."

"You know," I snapped. "You know, Luke Belka. We're alone. We're alone, and nobody's coming."

"We can't..."

"We're alone and you're going to leave me even more alone. You're going to go and everything hurts, Luke. I can't follow you anymore. I can't. I just..."

"I'm sorry," Luke said. He took a shuddering step towards me, and for a second, my burdens lifted. I opened my arms. He was going to kneel with me. He was going to stay.

He turned away.

"Luke," I shouted, pushing myself to my feet. He kept walking, one foot in front of the other, head down. He headed towards the mountain. He was going. He was going to leave me, and I was going to be alone, truly alone.

Just the thought of it made my hands shake. I'd thought about it before, of course, but not really. Not as something that might happen. That Luke might choose to do to me.

The twisting in my gut, then, as Luke walked away from me, was very real.

I was going to die there, and I may well die alone. I wasn't going to be able to live for long without him. Even if I set up my little house, even if I made a home, I wouldn't live long. Not in a way that was recognisable as me, anyway. Not in a way that mattered.

I needed him.

I pushed myself to my feet. My breath shuddered and tears ran down my cheeks. I needed him.

He was getting further away. Soon, I wasn't going to be able to see him anymore. Soon, he was going to be too far away, and then what would I do? There was this entire planet and we were so small, so fragile. What if he fell? What if he hurt himself? He might lie out there for days before he died. I might look for him and never find him.

He needed me. Something was very wrong with him, very broken in him, but he needed me. If I let him walk away and something happened...

I stepped out into the rain. It mingled with the tears on my cheeks. I had to find him. I had to follow him.

I loved him.

I was stupid. I should have known it before. Should have known it when he made me my bed, when he smiled at me like he cared, the first time he kissed me. I never did though. I just thought we were the last people alive. I just thought...

I loved him. I wanted to be with him. Even if I could walk back to camp and be okay. Even if I could go back and make a house and live quietly until I passed away peacefully. Even if that was a thing I believed could happen, I could never do it. Not really. I'd rather follow him. I'd rather die holding his hand on the side of a stupid mountain.

I loved him.

I couldn't live without him because I loved him.

And what else was there left for me to do but love him. If loving Luke was the only thing I could manage with my miserable life, at least that'd be something. At least I could say I'd done something truly for myself.

The ground was uneven and the water wasn't making it any better. It was slow going, I couldn't see Luke ahead of me anymore. The rain got thicker, pouring from the sky. I was soaked to the bone but I didn't stop. I couldn't stop. I had to keep going, because, if I lost him, if I never saw him again...

I sobbed, clutched my gut, forced myself to keep going. I had to find him. I had to.

I had to tell him I loved him at least once. Even if, to him, I was only the person he was stuck here with. Even if he'd never choose me, he had to know I'd choose him. A million times, on any planet, with any other choice, I'd choose him. I'd choose him and his kindness, his friendship, the way he didn't seem to know how to give up on something. The way he believed right down to his core, even when it ended like this and he should have given up. I couldn't help loving that he still hoped, that he still cared.

The ground got steeper. I wasn't sure if my shaking was the panic or the cold any more. My feet were throbbing, each step was hell, but I pressed on. I couldn't leave him alone. I just couldn't.

Then, out in the rain, a figure. I'd found him. My breath caught. I'd found him. We were going to be together. Whatever happened, I was never letting go again.

It took me a few more steps to realise he was on his knees. My heart jolted at the sight. I pushed myself on, forced myself to move that little bit faster, forced my body to endure. He just knelt there, on his knees.

He looked like he'd given up.

He must have heard me desperately struggling over the stones as he turned. He saw me and he pushed to his feet. He seemed unsteady, uncertain. He took a step towards me, then another. Then he was running, as much as his own ruined feet would let him. I ran, as much as mine would let me. We crashed into each other on the side of the mountain. My arms locked around him, his around me. I dug my fingers into the flesh of his hips, clung to him, pressed my face into his shoulder.

This close, I realised he was sobbing too. Sobbing and clinging to me as though he were trying to press me into his skin and keep me there.

"I'm sorry," he sobbed. "I'm sorry. I don't know what to do."

My heart broke.

All this time, he'd been the one with the plan. He'd been the one who knew what to do. Now, I pressed closer to him. I let him lean on me. Let him crumble, his weight pulling us both down to the rough ground.

"It's okay, love," I whispered, clinging. "It's okay. You don't need to know any more. It's going to be okay."

He sobbed, but he didn't argue with me. Instead, he pulled me as close as he could, his large, rough body settling against mine. Bruised and scraped from the last few days. I lifted my hand and ran it along his side, his back.

The rain started to clear.

We lay there for a while. I closed my eyes and basked in the nearness of him. I pressed my arms into him, dug in my fingers just to feel the texture of his flesh, the muscles under his skin. He was perfect. He was prefect and beautiful and I'd done nothing to deserve him but he was mine anyway and I loved him. Whatever it took, from here on out, he was mine and I loved him.

"It's okay," I promised, knowing it was all empty words, running my hands over and over his body. "Things are going to be okay now. We'll work it out together. I swear, me and you, we can do this. Together."

"Together," he repeated, though, I wasn't sure he understood it. I shifted us, settling on my ass. A rock dug into me uncomfortably but I was too tired to care. Luke pulled back a little and looked me in the eye. His eyes were red rimmed with massive bags under them. His beard was a disaster. He'd lost weight this last week. He was the most beautiful man I'd ever seen.

I leaned in and pressed a soft kiss to his lips. He gently returned it. It felt like a new first kiss. A new start.

"Alex," he said, voice chipped. "I don't..."

"Shh, it's alright." I patted his hair, pulling him against me and encouraging him to settle in my arms.

The rain carried on but that was good, it hid our tears. It wasn't like we could get any wetter anyway. We were both soaked through to the bone. I knew I should move him, should get us both up, but I couldn't. I didn't want to.

The sun was setting and Luke was heavy in my arms. They felt heavy themselves, so I just adjusted us, letting the rain fall and Luke's body warm me as the sun crept lower and lower, the twin moons making an appearance.

I looked down at Luke. He rested on my shoulder, eyes closed. Then I looked out at the world.

Our ship stood proud, an embarrassment against the beauty of this new place. This new place full of trees. Tree and trees, as far as we could see.

And maybe I hadn't given up hope, not completely, as a few more tears found their ways to the corners of my eyes at the sight of it. A little something in my soul pressed me to go higher, see better, to carry on and prove to myself it wasn't true, there was still human life out there.

In my arms, Luke shifted. I pressed a kiss to his forehead.

The rain was almost gone now. I dragged myself out from under Luke and he stirred, turning to look at me. He looked eerie in the half-light of the setting sun and I leaned over, kissed his rain-soaked skin. He was mine. I was going to make him safe. I was going to make this okay for us.

We had a tarp we'd been sleeping on, but I spread it over us that night. I knew I should force us to get changed, but the heat was already rising; we'd be dry by the time I managed it judging by how heavy my limbs were and how slow my movements. Instead I dragged the pack over and used it as a pillow, tucked the tarp around us, and settled Luke against me. He went quietly, easily. It broke my heart a little but I knew it'd get better. From here, it had to get better.

Maybe tomorrow he'd want to fight on. Maybe he'd be ready to go back. Either way, I was going with him.

Either way, we were doing it together.

Chapter Thirty-Two

IN THE MORNING light, nothing had changed. We were cold, wet, aching, part way up a small mountain with the only sign of life on the horizon, the ship we'd come in. It felt ironic to think of that as a sign of life given we were the only living things that had crawled out of it.

It was maybe better not to think about it at all.

Luke woke when I pushed at him, but something in him had clearly shifted, broken. He sat there staring out at the world, face blank. He didn't seem heartbroken by it or elated. He just seemed quiet, resigned.

I made up a couple of pouches of nutrient paste. It was probably more than I should have, but I did it anyway. We were going to need the energy. We'd not make it back to our little shelter without eating the local food. Luke was just going to have to accept that now. He didn't even seem to be thinking about it as he took the food from me and ate.

When we'd eaten, I helped him strip. We'd brought some changes of clothes and he let me help him into the new ones. He let me dry him carefully with another set of his dry clothes, these dirtier and more battered. He let me ease his feet out of his boots and dry them, then wrap them. He was polite. He smiled uncertainly at me a few times, then seemed to lapse back into silence, staring at the horizon and hoping for something to change.

I took care of myself, then. I stripped down, used the same dirty shirt to dry myself, then dressed again. I addressed the problem of my feet. Once out of my boots, they were swollen, blistered, aching, but not as terrible as I'd imagined them. I wrapped them in strips of cloth for support and eased them into clean socks, then back into my boots shockingly easily.

Then I stood and surveyed my domain.

We were alone. As far as we could see. We were above the tree line, maybe as high as our ship, there in its charred clearing. A tiny mountain of its own.

I looked at it and I knew what we had to do.

I went and sat beside Luke. He stirred a little, leaned into my side. I picked up his hand and squeezed it. He was so warm. So close.

"Okay," I said, trying to keep my voice firm. "We're going to climb."

"We don't have to," he said. "You were right. You are right. There's nobody."

"I know," I say. There's no point denying it. "But we came this far. We're going to climb, and we're going to see. We're going to be absolutely sure, one hundred percent. We're not going all the way to the top, but we're sure as hell going higher than the ship. I don't want this to be a thing we could have avoided by knocking a hole in a wall and looking out. We're going to walk around the mountain, and then we'll know. And then we'll go home and decide what to do from there."

"You're sure?" he asked. He looked tired, resigned, and for a second, I questioned it. For a second, I thought about heading back, about taking him away from the harsh reality of this place and letting him carry on pretending. Letting myself carry on pretending.

"We're going to see," I said, firmly. "It's really not that big a mountain. We can camp at the top tonight and then..."

"Then we go home," he finished for me. He still didn't sound convinced, but he stood and reached for my hand and I let him take it. Let him squeeze my fingers.

"Then we go home," I agreed.

Chapter Thirty-Three

THE TOP OF the mountain was almost anti-climactic. We climbed for the day, stopping to rest more than we had been before. Luke let me set the pace. He didn't try to talk, just kept stopping to look back. His hope seemed to fade a little bit more each time we saw nobody.

The only mountain I'd ever climbed before was Snowden, which we'd done as a training exercise. This one was higher, but the climb itself wasn't much worse. We climbed until lunch, we ate, we climbed again. We stopped at a relatively level place as afternoon turned to evening.

There was still no life to be seen. We sat there, silently, and looked out. We were going to live on that planet for the rest of our lives. We were going to die there. We looked over it and I reached out and took Luke's hand. He squeezed my fingers, forced a distant smile, and leaned into my shoulder.

"I love you," I said. Blurted might be a better way to describe it. For a second, he looked shocked, then he smiled and it felt, this time, like something in the smile was more genuine.

"I love you too."

And he leaned in to kiss me.

Chapter Thirty-Four

IN THE LIGHT of the morning, we walked around the mountain. We looked down, saw the rivers, the lakes, the masses and masses of trees. I scanned the horizon for sea, but I couldn't even glimpse it.

In the afternoon, we sat facing our ship. I took out my sketchbook and copied down the landscape. I took some photographs, too, but there was something more satisfying about running my pencil over the paper, tracing the line of the river that ran by our shelter, feeling its curves under my fingers. It looped and meandered and we'd definitely be able to take some pretty safe shortcuts getting back.

From up there, our ship seemed small. Everything we'd done to this planet seemed small. I looked out, and I imagined the planet thousands of years in the future, when we were gone.

I wondered if there'd ever be a civilisation. If anyone would dig up the remains of our ship and wonder.

I don't know what Luke thought about. He sat and silently looked out. His face was carefully neutral. I let him be. It was a lot. Too much, really. That kind of isolation, it wasn't something the human heart was meant to handle.

I held him that night while he slept and I thought. Thought about our lives and about our futures. The weight of his head on my shoulder, the tangle of his fingers in my T-shirt, they gave me hope.

The next morning, we started the walk home.

Chapter Thirty-Five

"YOU KNOW," I said, shielding my eyes against the sun. "I think if we cut across here tomorrow, we could cut out a loop of the river, and that'll save us a few days."

The silence hung for a few minutes. I glanced back at Luke. He blinked at me, as though he was trying to draw me into focus, then nodded. "Yeah, sure. That sounds good. We should try."

"Luke..."

"I know, I'm sorry," he said, wincing. He'd hardly been the best conversation partner for the past few days and I was trying, I really was. I'd been checking on my map and my photos and I'd guided us through one successful diversion already, but it had felt like such a risk. Setting out into the forest like that. If I'd been wrong...

It had felt more pressing at the time. It had felt like Luke was hardly there at all. Like, if I hadn't led him by the hand, he'd have just laid down up there on that mountain and not moved again.

Things were getting better. They were.

"Hey," he said, stepping up to me and bumping shoulders. "You've looked at the maps and the pictures, you won't lead us wrong. I trust you."

Heat crawled up my neck. "What if I have it wrong? I'm not a trained cartographer. Maybe we should just follow the river. I..."

"Alex, are we going to get lost?"

"No," I said, biting my lip. I was pretty certain. If we were where I thought we were—and the crook in the river here was pretty distinctive—then even if we got off trajectory and walked quite a way out, we should still hit the river doubling back on itself.

"I trust you," Luke repeated. He grabbed my hand and squeezed it. "And I'm ready to be home."

My heart fluttered a little at the idea Luke might think of our place on this planet as home. I felt like that about it, sure, but to know Luke did too... Some of my happiness must have been showing, because he leaned in and kissed my cheek and my heart fluttered again.

I hoped I never stopped feeling so in love with him.

"Anyway, we'll camp here tonight," I said, glancing away. "I don't think we're too far from twilight and I don't want to stumble around in the forest with the light fading."

"Sure," Luke agreed easily. He set his backpack down and I did, too, glad to be relieved of the weight. It was getting lighter, of course, as we ate our supplies, but we were also getting weaker, and we both badly needed a rest. When we got back to camp, I was going to wrap us both up in blankets and keep us in bed for a week.

After all, it wasn't like we had anything else to do.

I crouched down by my pack. For now, we had to focus on the journey.

"Here," I said, pulling my water canister out and brandishing it in his direction. "Go top up the water. I'll set the camp."

"Sure," he agreed, accepting the water canister then stooping to free his own. Once he was distracted, I dragged our bags a little further back into the trees, finding a comfortable-looking clearing. This had become my job. Luke was getting better at following instructions, but he still wasn't all there. The first night back in the trees, I'd asked him to set camp and he'd just looked lost.

It had broken my heart.

I pulled the groundsheet we'd brought from Luke's bag and spread it out so we'd have somewhere dry to sit. We had sleeping bags, too, and I liberated them. We'd given up on using them like you were meant to pretty early on, and I arranged them into their usual configuration, one laid out like a mattress with the other over it. Our little bed that we could crawl into together and press against each other.

The stove was in my pack and I took it out and then fished around for some nutrient powder. We didn't have much left. I took it out to count. Two pouches in my bag, six in Luke's. Even if we ate sparingly, it would only last a few more days.

I put them aside and set up the fuel instead. Something else we were running out of.

It'd be okay, we'd make it back to camp. We might just have to be creative.

"Hey."

I looked up. Luke was standing awkwardly at the edge of the campsite, palms cupped. He smiled at me hesitantly then lowered his palms and opened them.

He was holding a handful of berries: the rich blue ones that I recognised because I'd picked them near our landing site. I'd shown them to him, though I hadn't thought he was paying attention. I'd tested them. It made my heart flutter to see him there holding them. I now knew he had been paying attention to me.

"These are the right ones, right? I saw them down by the river's edge, and I was sure..."

"Yes," I squeaked. "I didn't think you were paying attention to me when I brought them back."

"I always pay attention to you." He said it so earnestly, so pleased with himself, I had to climb to my feet and kiss him. I took his face between my palms and pressed our lips together gently, tenderly. I enjoyed the way he sighed against my skin.

Then I took the berries from him, his fingers already stained with their juices. I hesitated then brought one to my mouth. They were fine. I was sure they were going to be fine. I knew their exact chemical composition. I was damn good at the analysis I did, which was what had gotten me on this mission to start with. They were fine.

But if they weren't, I was going first.

I popped a berry into my mouth.

It was tarter than I'd expected, but still good. I think, after the blandness of the nutrient paste, anything would have been manna. I closed my eyes and let the tastes of it fill my mouth, just giving myself a second to fully appreciate it.

Then I opened my eyes and selected another berry. I held it up to Luke's lips, and he opened for me, let me place it on his tongue, then hummed in pleasure as he ate it. I couldn't resist kissing him again, chasing the taste on his lips. I squashed my handful of berries as I pulled him close, the ones in his hands dropped as he wrapped my arms around me and pulled me to him.

"Thank you," I panted into his ear. "Just, thank you. I needed that."

"I should have listened to you earlier," he told me, all sweet sincerity. "I should have trusted you."

"You're listening now."

"Yes," he agreed. "I'm listening now."

"Good. Then let's go down to the river and pick some dinner."

He chuckled, leaned in again to kiss me with his hands pressing into my hips. I might have tried to drag him down into bed with me, but I really was tired and hungry. Hungry enough to gently push him away and lead him back down to the water. He'd left our canteens there and he filled them while I picked fruit using my T-shirt as a bag of sorts. I spotted another berry I'd tested and brought some of them along too.

That night, we gorged ourselves on the native food. The other berries were small, hard, and sweet almost like candy. We savoured them, feeding them to each other. We kissed a lot, gentle and slow. After all, there was no need to rush.

I fell asleep with the tastes of berries and of Luke lingering on my lips.

Chapter Thirty-Six

WE CAME AROUND a bend to a lake. Well, maybe more of a pond. But it was a hot day and the water looked cool and deep enough to swim in. My feet were aching and my back hurt, but we were over half way home by my reckoning, which was enough to keep my feeling light.

Luke rounded the corner behind me and stopped, looking out over the water's surface. He blinked at it, then glanced at me as though he wanted to check in that something was okay. I just shrugged and he dropped his bag and made his way down to the water, kneeling on the bank and scooping handfuls of it into his mouth and over his head. I watched him, tracing the tails of water down the back of his neck.

When I glanced up again it was noon. We might easily do a few more miles if we carried on walking.

"Alex?" I turned around. Luke was crouched there, looking up at me. "The water's cool."

That was apparently all I needed. I dropped my pack and went down to join him. My knees pressed into the soft moss at the edge of the water and I put my hands below the cold, refreshing surface.

I wanted to swim. I wanted it so badly. We should have walked more but...

"Look," Luke said, gesturing up the bank a little way. "Aren't those your favourite?"

I looked up. Yes, they were. We'd tried a variety of the berries I recognised by now and these seemed to be the richest, the sweetest. I started to salivate at the sight of them.

It wouldn't hurt too much just to stop, would it? To just enjoy some time in the sun?

I looked at Luke and he was looking back at me. There was something hopeful in his eyes and I realised with a start he was thinking the same thing I was. He wanted to stay here, but he was waiting for me to make the decision. He was leaving this in my hands.

It was oddly humbling.

"Yes," I said. "They're my favourites. Do you think we could maybe rest for the rest of today?"

"I mean," Luke said, glancing out at the water, "my feet are pretty sore. I know you want to get home, but maybe it'd be better if we rest for a day? We'll feel better tomorrow."

"We will," I agreed, reaching over to squeeze Luke's arm in reassurance. "You do know I'm not in charge right now though, right? I mean, it's not my choice to stop and if I don't stop, you can say you want to. You aren't following me."

"I mean, I kind of am." Luke shrugged. "I dragged us out here. You never even wanted to come. Getting back as quickly as we can—"

"Luke," I interrupted, "we're a team. We're doing this together."

"I just... I was selfish. I don't want to be. I want you to be happy. I want to make you happy."

"I am," I promised, reaching over to grab his hand. "I mean, my feet hurt and I completely agree with you that I need a rest, but I'm happy, Luke."

He seemed to contemplate that for a second really taking it in, then he nodded. He smiled softly when he did, like I'd given him something precious. Like he hadn't known before that just being around him was special to me.

"Luke, you do know I love you."

"I... yes. I mean, you told me before. You were upset though. We were on the mountain and I shouldn't have left you. I just..."

"I love you," I said, promising myself right then and there I was going to say it every day from then on.

"You too," Luke said, smiling. "I love you too. I think, if I'd landed with anyone else, this would have been hell. And, I mean, don't get me wrong, this is far from perfect, but every time I want to give in, I think about you and everything you've done. I think about how you made us a home out here. I think about how much you've tried to make life better. I think about how you've supported me and cared for me even when I was being an ass. I love you. I like to think, even if we'd landed fine, I'd have found you eventually anyway. I can't imagine not having you now."

I leaned over and pressed my face into his neck. His skin was warm and perfect to hide my tears against. His arms slid around me, hands splaying across my back and rubbing soft, slow circles into my skin.

He loved me. He really loved me.

"Hey," he said eventually, voice soft against my hair. "Don't make a noise, but just look up across the clearing."

I did, slowly.

There was a creature there.

A large variant on the lizard-like things I'd seen. It was brown and purple and it had four eyes, two on either side of a squat head. Its body was long and slender, stocky limbs held it up. It leaned down, unconcerned, to drink from the pool. We watched it, hardly daring to breathe. It was maybe the size of a large housecat, which made it by far the largest thing I'd seen since I got to the planet.

There was so much to see, and for a second my heart was overwhelmed with the wonder of it. With the idea I might live here forever and still not understand all of this beautiful new world we'd fallen into.

I was going to get a chance to understand it. Luke and I were going to have a life here.

The creature turned and moved, surprisingly quickly for its bulk, back into the brush. We watched it go, then sighed.

"I knew it," I said, almost afraid not to whisper in case it came back. "I knew there had to be some larger creatures out there. The fruits, they'd only evolve if there was something eating them and it's not beetles. I wonder if that's the biggest or if there's more. I haven't seen any signs of any creatures eating each other yet but—"

"Alex," Luke interrupted, his voice soft and amused. "Come on, love. Let's swim."

I laughed. Yes, I was getting ahead of myself. I stood quickly and grabbed my T-shirt, pulling it up over my head. The air felt good on my skin and I knelt down again to free my feet from my boots. It took a while to unwrap them but they felt good too, exposed to the fresh air, and I took a few more minutes just to stretch them out. Then I finished stripping easily. Luke was already out on the lake so I eased into the water and joined him.

For a little while I just swam around, enjoying the stretch in my muscles. It was nice to move in a way that wasn't walking. Soon, though, even that was too hard and I let myself float instead, drifting over to where Luke was watching me.

"Hey," I said, turning to smile at him. "I love you."

"Love you too," he said easily. "You feeling cooler?"

"Yes." I was feeling a million times better. The aches in my arms and legs were gone and I felt loose and happy.

"Good," Luke said, then grabbed me and dunked me under the water. I came up sputtering, flailing, and looking for revenge. The next half hour or so consisted of us fighting our way around the lake, splashing and chasing each other, stealing quick kisses each time we managed to trap the other one, then swimming away again.

It was the most fun I'd had in a long time.

Eventually, exhaustion won out and we dragged our wet, naked bodies up onto the bank. Luke was apparently in better shape than me because he headed to the bags and brought out the ground sheet so I didn't have to lie on the grass. I crawled up and sprawled out on it, closing my eyes and letting the sun bake me dry.

I maybe slept, I certainly dozed, and the next time I was fully away, Luke was sitting by my side. I lay there and watched him for a moment. His skin was golden under the sun. His arms were so strong, so well-muscled. He was built so beautifully, I really was lucky. Not that I wouldn't have loved him if he was ugly. It was just joyous he was a beautiful person and had a beautiful body.

I rolled over a little to watch him better. He was still naked, reclining and looking out lazily over the lake. I could imagine long afternoons spent like this at our little lake next to our waterfall with a little house up above. Just the two of us making the most of this place we'd been given.

He looked down at me and smiled, then offered me one of the berries he was eating. I opened my mouth to let him place it on my tongue, then grabbed his wrist, holding his hand in place so I could lick it clean of juices.

That certainly made him take notice. He turned to face me more fully, then offered me more fruit, letting me eat it from his fingers again and diligently lick them clean for him by pulling them into my mouth and swirling my tongue around them until his eyes went dark and unfocused.

"Alex," he said, voice low and heavy, and I let go of his wrist to move up onto my knees instead. I took his face in my hands and leaned in, kissing him deeply and passionately. He folded under me obligingly, laying back on the ground and letting me press kisses along his jaw, down his neck. He gasped, his hands coming round to splay over my hips.

It was so good, lying there in the sun with him below me, that I relaxed into him. I let him take my weight so our skin touch and I could feel him below me. He felt so good.

"I love you," I whispered between kisses, and he whimpered when I did. I wondered if he'd needed to hear it as much as I did. If he'd needed me to say it, waited for me. I was never going to make him wait again. Not for that anyway.

I drew out the kissing—though it was clear that wasn't going to be the end of what we did together—until he got frustrated enough to roll me over and press me down into the ground, his toned, strong body oddly gentle with mine like he was scared he was going to break me. He caught my wrists but then just kissed the insides of them and let them free again. He kissed down my arms and along my collarbone, under my chin and down my neck. I was achingly hard by then and squirming beneath him, but he ignored that, taking his time kissing me.

And why not, we had all the time in the world. The rest of our lives. We were alone, but we were free. No more obligation. No more pleasing others.

Eventually, he worked his way across my stomach and found his way to my cock, hard and heavy between my legs. He pressed a few gentle, tentative kisses there first like he expected to be pushed away. Like I ever would!

Permission granted, he went to town. Luke was the kind of man committed 110 percent to whatever he was doing and he brought that kind of dedication to sucking cock. The hot, wetness of his mouth, the gentle support of his hand, the brush of his wilderness beard over my thighs; it was all overwhelming.

I found myself thrashing on the ground, mewling as I thrusted up into his mouth and chanted, over and over again, "I love you. I love you. I love you." He moaned when I did, the feeling of that vibrating right down to my core and shocking more words into tumbling out of my mouth until suddenly it was too much.

"Luke," I gasped. He pulled back, finishing me with a few quick strokes. I gasped as I spilled out, keening his name. He leaned over me, watched me like he couldn't believe I was real, like I was the best thing he'd ever seen.

Then he reached down and wrapped a hand around his own cock, hanging swollen and beautiful between us. I made a needy sound and went to bat his hand away so I could do it, but the orgasm had left me uncoordinated.

"It's okay," Luke said, voice thick and desperate. "It's okay, Alex. Please, just let me do this. Just let me come. You can do it next time."

"Yeah," I said. And the time after and a million times after that, I thought "Please, Luke. Come for me. Come on love, do this for me."

"Yes," he said, lifting up to a whine at the end, and that was it for him. He came over me, then collapsed, panting into my shoulders. I brought my arms around him and sighed, then leaned in and kissed him until he calmed, and his body was still again.

I loved him.

He was mine.

We were going to be okay.

Chapter Thirty-Seven

THE CAMP WAS much as we'd left it. We stumbled in late one afternoon, managing to check things were habitable and to drag some mattresses over from the ship before we crawled into bed and finally relaxed. The first few days back were spent mostly sleeping, occasionally waking to kiss or fuck or whisper how much we loved each other before drifting back to sleep.

On the third, or maybe the fourth day, I woke up to find Luke sitting beside me in the bed, the doors thrown open so the sun could get in as best it could and a notepad on his lap. He was frowning at it.

"What are you doing?" I asked blearily.

"Planning," he said, lowering his pencil to the paper then lifting it away again. "Preliminary, really. Just as an outline for our ideas."

"Planning what?" I asked, rolling over. He smiled down at me then put his pad aside to lean in for a kiss. I let him, but I also didn't want to get distracted and, after a few seconds, I pushed him away again. "Planning what?"

"A house," he admitted, grabbing the pad again. "I know we're meant to do it together but I was thinking…"

I smiled. How could I not love him being enthusiastic for building us a life together? "Go on, then, love. Show me."

"Here," he said, tilting the page towards me. The plan was rudimentary, but clear. A one-storey house built off the ground, which was probably a good idea even if the area I wanted to build in hadn't flooded last time. A porch ran around its outside. It looked comfortable. Quaint.

"Windows," I said. "I want lots of windows." He jotted that down at the side. "And maybe, not right away but later, a swing on the porch. I've never had anything like that."

"It's very American," Luke said, then wrote the note down. "I haven't laid out the inside yet, but I figure we only need the basics: a bedroom, living and kitchen area, bathroom. We can expand if we need more space later, but since it's only you and me..."

There was a tinge of sadness there, but I didn't let it get a hold, rather tugged him down to kiss me again. It was just for me and him, but that didn't mean it was any less full of love.

"It sounds beautiful."

He smiled and tumbled me back into the sheets, startling a laugh out of me. We had a lot ahead of us. We'd have to track down materials, hope that the wood was good for building. We'd have to actually build the thing, and that would probably involve a lot of arguing. Eventually, we were going to have to deal with the ship and the fact that those stasis chambers were running on a very limited supply of fuel. We'd have to make a decision about planting crops and contaminating the planet versus hunting for native plants that'd meet our nutritional needs. We'd have to see what winter was like on this planet, if it ever came. There were going to be a million places to explore and a million jobs to do.

But, for that morning, I let Luke tumble me back into the bed. I kissed him and I made sure he knew I loved him.

In the end, nothing was more important than that.

About the Author

Emmalynn Spark is a male/male romance author from England. She spends her time crying about fictional boys, eating as many different cakes and she can and complaining about the weather.

Email EmmalynnSpark@gmail.com

Twitter: @EmmalynnSpark

Website: www.emmalynnspark.com

Other books by this author

"Deathless" within *Once Upon a Rainbow, Volume Two*

Also Available from NineStar Press

Connect with NineStar Press

www.ninestarpress.com

www.facebook.com/ninestarpress

www.facebook.com/groups/NineStarNiche

www.twitter.com/ninestarpress

www.tumblr.com/blog/ninestarpress